KIM WHATMORE lives in H
designs gardens. Since reading A
spent time working for charity. S
and travelled.

CW00401371

KIM WHATMORE lives in Hampshire with her two cats and
... Since reading Anthropology at university she has
spent time working for charity. She has also done research, written
and travelled.

TABITHA
GOES
EAST

KIM
WHATMORE

SilverWood

Published in 2021 by SilverWood Books

SilverWood Books Ltd
14 Small Street, Bristol, BS1 1DE, United Kingdom
www.silverwoodbooks.co.uk

ISBN 978-1-80042-103-5 (paperback)
ISBN 978-1-80042-104-2 (ebook)

British Library Cataloguing in Publication Data
A CIP catalogue record for this book is
available from the British Library

Page design and typesetting by SilverWood Books

For John and my mum and dad

ACKNOWLEDGEMENTS

It's been nearly twenty years since I started working on *Tabitha Goes East*. Firstly, I'd like to thank Josie Pearse, my writing coach, for all her patient, hard work. I'd also like to thank my tutor Richard Skinner at The Faber Academy, as well as my tutor group there and all my dear friends and family for supporting me through what has been a long and often arduous process: in particular Steven Hickling, Lou Cooper, Lucinda Palmer, Philippa Hanscombe, Georgina d'Angelo, Katie Campbell, Chris Gangadin, Sophie Guiness, Emma Hudson, Claudia Nye, Caitlin Smail, Katie James, Nina Fison, Tim Harding, Cathy Squire, Carol Qirreh, Sascha Dutton-Forshaw and Nicola Hok. Finally, I'd like to thank all the team at SilverWood for publishing it.

CHAPTER 1

The tigress opened one eye. Stretching her foreleg, she examined her forepaw. Black velvet pads to die for – no doubt about it. Bounding out of bed, she dressed. It was five forty in the morning. She'd overslept, and how. The elephants, Jeffrey and Gloria, were coming to pick her up at six. She was late – very. She pulled on her cropped white T-shirt and blue and black striped North Face fleece as fast as she could, and put on her small white knickers, as well as her long black socks, with beige combat pants over the top. She didn't wear a bra. No need – her small breasts were perfectly formed. Lastly she slipped on her Merrells – for which, read expensive beige suede slip-ons – and did her teeth, especially her canines.

Just as she was flossing, there was a knock at the door. She opened up. Gloria stood on the front path. Even though Gloria was an elephant, she was wearing a twinset in pale pink cashmere fluffed at the edges, pearls and a tweed skirt.

'Good morning, darling girl,' she said.

'Good morning, Gloria,' said Tabitha.

'Is that all you're taking?' said Gloria, pointing to Tabitha's small green bag.

'That and my rucksack,' said Tabitha. She had bought the small green bag from Heal's years ago and thought it fitting that she should now be taking such a stylish, if diminutive, piece of luggage on such a grand tour of southern India. 'Can I offer you a cup of anything?'

'That's kind of you, but no. I think we had better get going. Jeffrey's waiting in the car.'

Tabitha picked up her bag, said a cursory goodbye to her pet cat Twinkle, who was pregnant, and waltzed out of the house. She was followed by the elephant, also waltzing. On hind legs, they waltzed down the street. Jeffrey, also on hind legs and doing a jig, was scraping ice from the back windscreen of the car.

'Let me help you with that,' he said to Tabitha, taking her bag. The two elephants and the tigress piled into the car. They drove to Heathrow. When they got there the tigress, who was sitting in the back, was careful, while getting out of the car, not to damage the front seat with her claws any more than she had already done. Once outside, the elephants said their goodbyes. Tabitha looked away. Even though the elephants had been married for years, she wanted to give them their privacy. Also, any sign of conjugal love set Tabitha off. She wanted to cry.

'Are you all right there?' said Gloria.

'Never better,' Tabitha lied. 'I've just got something in my eye.'

Tabitha and Gloria set off for the terminal. They got to the doors, which opened automatically. The animals were taken aback. The tigress looked to one side, then the other. No more doors, she thought. Thank goodness for that. Then she stepped over the recessed track that marked the edge of the building and proffered Gloria her paw. Taking it, Gloria stepped gingerly over the track and entered the building.

The tour guide who was standing at the SwissAir desk was wearing a blue canvas jacket and a pink and white striped shirt with a pair of white chinos. He was also sporting a pair of scuffed deck shoes and had a yellow embroidered handbag slung over his shoulder. He saw the animals before they saw him. He beamed. The tigress frowned. She was unused to travelling with men, and was realising the implications of what she had done by signing up for a tour led by a man. Yikes, she thought. I'm going to have to keep my head down here.

'Welcome on tour. I'm Andrew, your guide for the next three weeks,' he said in dulcet tones.

'Why, thank you,' said Gloria. 'I'm Gloria and this is Tabitha.'

Tabitha, who had immediately warmed to his tones, kept schtum and allowed her bag to trundle down her forearm and swing to the floor. By chance it landed at Andrew's feet. Like a gauntlet, challenging him to take me on tour, she thought.

'You do travel lightly,' he said. Tabitha was just about to reply to what she perceived to be his compliment when a pelican came in to land. She was wearing a billowing white shirt tucked into a pair of well-tailored but tightly fitting pin-striped trousers, and her buxom lines mimicked those of her variously sized but matching grey suitcases.

'Kathleen,' said the pelican in an Irish lilt. 'You must be Andrew. Delighted, I'm sure. Sorry I'm late. I do hope I haven't delayed you.'

You may not have delayed us but you certainly have kept us waiting, thought the tigress. She looked down. In contrast to the pelican's attire, which looked as if it had just been flown in by the dry cleaners, hers was covered in cat hair.

'If you'd like to check your luggage,' said Andrew, 'we can go through to departures when the others arrive.'

'Who do you think he means by the "others"?' whispered the tigress to the elephant.

'They must be the other meditators who are joining us on tour,' whispered Gloria.

When the others did arrive, they included a rhino with bouffant grey hair, who put in an appearance wearing a floral print dress in a mauve colour that looked to the tigress as if it must have come from Marks & Spencer, as well as two bison and two buffalo. Andrew didn't introduce them all to one another, which Tabitha found odd, seeing as they were all going on holiday together. In fact, she found it so odd that she thought about legging it. Then she caught sight of Andrew looking earnestly over the Heathrow horizon – for stragglers, she supposed. How considerate, she thought.

'We can go through now,' he said, and with that the tigress, normally so independent, fell into line.

CHAPTER 2

On the first flight from London to Zurich Tabitha sat next to the elephant, who in turn was sitting next to the rhino. The elephant put on her pince-nez midway down her trunk and started to do the crossword. When she had finished, Tabitha, who wanted to be the elephant's new best friend on tour because she thought her a kind woman, started to tell the elephant her life story.

'I was born within the sound of Bow bells,' she said. 'Makes me a blue-blooded cockney.'

'Where does the blue blood come in?' said Gloria.

'My great-great-great-grandfather, the Earl of Dudley, had an affair with his serving maid. She became pregnant. To save face – his face – he married her off to the local publican.'

'Presumably your great-great-great-grandfather was married at the time.'

'Yes,' said the tigress emphatically. In fact, she was thinking, Oh my God, I hadn't thought about my great-great-great-grandfather's wife, nor about the serving maid for that matter. I was only thinking about my great-great-great-grandfather's bad behaviour and how that gave our family aristocratic status. How awfully unfeminist of me.

The elephant turned to the rhino. I must have blown it on the new best friend front, thought the tigress.

'Are you on tour?' said the elephant to the rhino.

'Yes,' said the rhino.

'Have you been on tour before?'

'Yes, to the North with Andrew and Babaji.'

'Who's Babaji?'

'Andrew's assistant.'

'What's he like?' said Tabitha.

'Who?' said the rhino proprietarily. As if she doesn't know who I'm talking about, thought the tigress.

'Andrew, of course,' said Tabitha.

'Oh, him. Oh, he likes to get up early and keep going all day.'

The tigress's heart sank. She liked to get up late and take rests while exploring. In spite of his earnest looks, considerate nature and dulcet tones, he sounded a bit too militaristic for her liking. The elephant went on to introduce herself and Tabitha to the rhino, who was called Rhonda and who, as Gloria soon discovered, came from Llandudno.

CHAPTER 3

In Zurich's international transfer lounge, the tigress was sitting next to the elephant on a black leather sofa and watching as Andrew and the other animals were meandering along the black marble concourse, making their way in and out of various shops and eateries. Andrew doesn't look like the kind of guy who knows where he's going, thought the tigress. Much less like a militaristic leader than I expected him to be. Could be of interest?

On the plane from Zurich to Mumbai, the animals reclined their seats and slept.

CHAPTER 4

The flight landed at just after midnight, local time. The animals were approaching the arrivals hall.

'Always the same, these so-called "Third World" airports,' said Tabitha to Gloria, looking at the peeling black paint at the base of the peppermint-green columns that supported the roof, and at the upturned edges of the linoleum tiles.

'Why do you say "so-called"?' asked Gloria.

'I once did a course in the epidemiology of ageing at the London School of Hygiene & Tropical Medicine. At the beginning of the course, we were asked to define "First" and "Third" World. Many of the words we used were the same.'

At passport control the tigress noticed the female bison talking to Andrew. She had a tuft of dark hair and was wearing a grey tracksuit, with the name of a football club emblazoned in pink capital letters across her chest, and trainers. Her mouth continuously opened and shut. His mouth rarely opened. Tabitha concluded that she was the more talkative of the two. What she didn't realise then was that she wanted to be the one talking to Andrew.

Outside the terminal there was a tangled mass of trolleys. The tigress pushed her trolley around it and crossed the road to a car park where there was a bus that looked like a Black Maria, other than that it was grey and had orange checked curtains bunched at the windows. Hotel staff jumped out of the bus and adorned the animals with giant flower garlands made from marigolds. Unfortunately, there weren't enough garlands to go round, and Andrew and Tabitha remained unadorned. Tabitha didn't mind, because she liked being in the same boat as Andrew. The hotel staff began loading suitcases into the back of the bus. Tabitha helped out. This also made her feel like she was in the same boat as Andrew because he was staff, so to speak. When she'd finished loading suitcases, the tigress looked into the back of the bus. The bison and the buffalo had taken all the seats. For a moment, the tigress thought she and the other animals were going to have to walk to the hotel, and her heart sank. Then Andrew hailed a taxi. It appeared as if from nowhere. The tigress, the elephant, the pelican and the rhino piled into the back. Andrew got into the front next to the driver.

'To the Taj,' he said. He didn't mean the Taj Mahal, of course. He meant the Taj President, which was the name of the hotel they were staying in for the first couple of nights.

As they drove away from the airport, the light from the orange street lamps penetrated the back of the cab, casting strange shadows over their legs.

Not far from the airport, a lungi-clad man emerged from a cardboard shack and stoked a fire. A little further on, they passed by grey stone mansions, like giants poised in line. The mansions were set back from the road behind baobab trees, the branches of which rose like stems and fell like curtains. The pelican spoke first.

'It's all very sophisticated here,' she said. There was an awkward silence.

Eventually, Andrew said, 'Hmmm.' Tabitha admired his equanimity. Had she been responding, she might have growled at the pelican, 'What does deprivation have to do round here to get itself noticed?'

'So what are we going to be doing on tour? Going clubbing?' said the pelican. 'Who else is single like me? Rhonda?'

Rhonda didn't answer. Instead she snorted, an embarrassed sort of a snort.

'What about you, Andrew?' A pelican asking a man if he was single was like a pelican asking a man to marry her, in the tigress's book. She could hardly believe her ears.

'I'm single,' said Andrew.

The tigress nearly fell out of the taxi. Most kind men she came across were spoken for. Was Kathleen going to ask her the same question? the tigress wondered.

'"Single" is not the right word,' she said, panicking. 'What about "available"?' But even that sounded like she meant 'available for a relationship', and she didn't want Andrew thinking that of her, not least at this early stage of their acquaintance. For her part, she wanted to remain mysterious for as long as possible. 'I know – what about "available to possibility"?' she continued. Not only had she hit upon a near-perfect phrase, she had also described a game they could all play – even Gloria, who sat demurely on the back seat, no doubt thinking of her husband; at least, that is what the tigress supposed she was thinking about.

The taxi pulled up outside the Taj President, which stood aglow, a golden skyscraper, in all its jaw-dropping, glittering splendour. Gloria got out of the taxi.

'I should never have come,' she said, rearranging her chignon.

'Whyever not?' said Tabitha, rearranging her flyaway bun.

'It's far too grand, and I'm already missing the cat.'

'What about your husband and your new home?'

'He won't be able to find the kitchen, let alone the fridge. I've written him instructions on Post-its I've left all over the house.'

How sweet, thought the tigress, biting back the tears. She followed the elephant through the revolving glass door at the top of the hotel steps and pulled herself together.

In the lobby they sat down on blue velveteen sofas with the other animals. As well as Kathleen, Gloria, Rhonda and Tabitha, there were Tracey and Eric, a couple of middle-aged bison from Hertfordshire, and Callum and Clodagh, a couple of middle-aged buffalo from County Cork.

'I'm sharing with Geraldine,' said Gloria, flapping her big ears.

'I know,' said Tabitha. 'I had hoped that when Hermione got sick you might have wanted to share with me.'

'Oh, darling girl, I'm so sorry. It didn't even occur to me. When Hermione fell sick, I just telephoned Geraldine. I don't know if you know but she came out early, five days ago in fact, with the hoolocks, Henry and Leticia, to attend satsang with Ramesh Balthezaar.'

As it happened, Tabitha did know Geraldine. As well as being a member of the meditation society to which Gloria and Tabitha also belonged, Geraldine was a glang, or half-domesticated yak, half-cow. As for the hoolocks, as well as being members of the meditation society to which Tabitha, Gloria and Geraldine also belonged, they were a type of gibbon or lesser ape. What she didn't know then, but desperately wanted to know, was who she was going to be sharing with. In some ways she thought it was most likely to be Kathleen because the two of them weren't as old as the others.

Andrew came over.

'I've got some revised itineraries for you,' he said. 'There'll be a test in the morning.'

A nervous titter ran round the group. They were all tired and ready for their beds. It was now two in the morning, local time, and it had been a long day. The last thing they wanted to do was to study revised itineraries, even if they had been written by their guide. He smiled. They sighed.

'Your key,' he said to Gloria. 'And yours,' he said to Kathleen. The tigress's heart sank. Kathleen had obviously paid the single supplement, and Tabitha was going to have to share with Rhonda. A tigress sharing with a rhino, I ask you, thought Tabitha. Getting up, she rolled her eyes skyward, as if to say to Andrew, Thank you for pulling me the short straw. Rhonda, who had, so the tigress thought, noted this exchange, got up, took their key and made straight for the lift. Tabitha followed. When they were in the lift, Tabitha asked Rhonda how she was. Rhonda didn't answer. Tabitha worried about her then. She was, after all, an elderly rhino who had flown halfway round the world to be in India with her beloved Andrew, or so the tigress supposed... Also, to the tigress, Rhonda seemed confused and disoriented.

'Which bed would you like?' said Tabitha to Rhonda in the room. Again Rhonda didn't answer. Tabitha put her rucksack on the bed nearest the window, ready to escape. There was a knock at the door. Rhonda rushed to open it. The porter brought in two enormous suitcases, both belonging to Rhonda, as well as Tabitha's small green bag.

'If you'd like to put that suitcase on the luggage rack and the other one on the floor beside it,' said Rhonda.

Tabitha was surprised to hear Rhonda, so obviously not talking to her, talking to the porter. Rhonda didn't go to tip him, though, so Tabitha did the honours; and, having done their ablutions, they turned in for the night.

CHAPTER 5

Next morning Tabitha drew back the uniform beige curtains of the Taj President. The window glass was tinted dark brown, turning the unexpectedly tall skyscrapers an odd shade of metallic green. She looked down. Far below, on terraces and in kitchens glimpsed through open windows, the Mumbai residents were enjoying their early morning rituals. Her own, a half hour of meditation, was followed by breakfast. When she began her half hour, Rhonda, sitting bolt upright in bed with a pained look upon her face, was also meditating. When she finished, Rhonda was nowhere to be seen. How rude, she thought. A rhino who leaves without so much as a by your leave. I ask you.

Tabitha went downstairs to the dining room. She couldn't see any other animal from the tour group so she went to the buffet, grabbed herself a cup of coffee and a croissant, and settled herself down at a square wooden table. When she'd finished, she handed her tray to a passing waiter.

'Cooee,' called Gloria from across the room. Getting up, Tabitha went over to join her. She was sitting with the rhino and the pelican beside a decorative piece of dark green trellis and a palm planted into a silver pot. 'Have you had your breakfast, darling girl?'

'Yes,' said Tabitha.

'Well, what did you have?'

Tabitha told the elephant, who was now flapping her big ears and waving her trunk, what she'd had.

'You can't have that now you're on the sub-continent. You must have something—well, a little more subcontinental. The samosas here are delicious. Waiter…' She ordered Tabitha a plate of samosas.

Their entry into the dining room coincided with Andrew's. This morning he was wearing an embroidered waistcoat over an off-white salwar kameez in cheesecloth, grey ribbed socks and brown leather sandals. If this is his idea of local dress, thought the tigress, then I'm going to get the giggles. She giggled.

Making straight for their table, he sat down next to the tigress. The elephant, the rhino and the pelican took their leave.

'I liked your postcard,' he said. 'Is it your garden?' She'd sent him the postcard along with her cheque for the full cost of the tour. The tigress pulled herself together.

'Yes,' she said, nearly getting the giggles again. 'I liked yours too.'

'Which one was that?'

'A golden temple silhouetted against a blue sky.'

'I know the one.'

'Imagine my disappointment when I turned it over,' she said. Andrew frowned.

'The temple was in Burma. I'd selected the wrong tour.'

Andrew smiled. 'I'm afraid duty calls. I'll see you in the lobby at nine thirty sharp for the first of our daily briefings.'

Bolting her samosas, Tabitha rushed back up to their room, where, before gathering her things for the day, she went to the loo. Her period had come early. Blaming the irregularity on international air travel, she inserted a tampon and rushed back downstairs to the lobby. Unusually, she was bang on time. Must be the Andrew effect, she thought.

'There's been a change of plan,' he said. 'Some of you,' he continued, staring directly at Rhonda, 'are keen to buy local clothing cheaply, so instead of going to Elephant Island this morning as planned, we'll be going there this afternoon. This morning I've organised for a bus to take you on a shopping expedition downtown.'

The bus, which was grey, was waiting in an acacia-lined street by the side of the hotel. The rhino, the pelican, the elephant, the bison, the buffalo, the tigress and various hotel staff, whom Tabitha imagined had been told to return the animals safely to the hotel on pain of death, hopped aboard. It wasn't long before they arrived at a grand department store covered in bamboo scaffolding. Tabitha hoped the scaffolding was strong enough to bear the weight of the men who toiled there and entered the store. In ladies wear she ran her paw, black velvet pads to die for, through a diaphanous grey salwar kameez with a neck embroidered in the colours of the rainbow. All of a sudden there was an almighty snort.

'The prices here are exorbitant. I'm going over the road to the marketplace,' said Rhonda. With that, the rhino left the store. Outside, there was a three-lane highway. Lorries, cars, tuk-tuks, bicycles, rickshaws and pedestrians stopped dead in their tracks as Rhonda, unperturbed, crossed over. In the corner of the marketplace there was a shop that Rhonda entered, followed by the rest of them. Salwar kameezes in an array of colours, which had been stacked neatly on shelves, took off and, as if piloted by salespeople, opened mid-air. They landed, perfectly displayed, on counters. The rhino pointed to a red one and a blue one.

'I'll try them both,' she said, making her way to a makeshift changing room. Moments later, she appeared from behind a white sheet, wearing the blue one, a little like the Virgin Mary.

Gloria and Tabitha walked down the side of the market. Tabitha caught sight of a miniature salwar kameez patterned in red, white and green. The colours of the Italian flag, she thought, strung up on what looks like a washing line. How sweet. Pointing to it, she said, 'How much?'

'For you, memsahib, seven hundred rupees,' said the stall-holder.

'That's just under a tenner,' Tabitha said to Gloria.

'Then you should get it,' she said.

Carefully, Tabitha extracted one blue note worth five hundred rupees and two brown notes worth a hundred rupees each from her money belt and paid. I say 'carefully' because once, at the start of a Turkish holiday, on account of not being au fait with the local currency, the tigress had made an inadvertent donation of fifty pounds to the Blue Mosque in Istanbul. The stallholder handed her her purchase in a brown paper bag. Gloria and Tabitha continued to walk down the side of the market. All of a sudden hotel staff swept the animals into a Chinese restaurant. Andrew was just inside the door.

'I take it you enjoyed your retail therapy,' he said. 'There are some faces over there you might recognise,' he continued. Tabitha looked over to the other side of the restaurant. Geraldine the glang and Henry the hoolock, both members of the meditation society to which Gloria the elephant, Hermione the heron, and Tabitha the tigress also belonged, were standing talking to one another. As Tabitha had last seen them at the meditation society in the vicinity of Barons Court and they were now such a long way from home, she wanted to kiss and hug them all at the same time.

Henry, the male hoolock, turned to her and said stiffly, 'I don't think you've met my wife, have you? Tabitha, this is Leticia. Leticia, Tabitha.'

The tigress shook Leticia's hand and noticed how peculiarly limp it was – Especially for a hoolock, she thought.

They sat down in booths on red leather banquettes. Their drinks, which had been ordered by the hoolock at the bar, soon arrived. Condensation ran down the sides of the glasses, leaving damp patches on the white paper tablecloth. There was an awkward silence. To alleviate it, Tabitha delved into the brown paper bag by her striped thigh and held up her new salwar kameez.

'Even you will have difficulty getting into that,' said Geraldine. Neither of the hoolocks spoke.

'It's for my niece, aged three,' said Tabitha.

On the ferry bound for Elephant Island, Tabitha took a photograph of the hoolocks asleep on one another's shoulders. Funny how hoolocks come on holiday and fall asleep, she thought. They must be tired. Depressed by their tedium and the impact it might have on the group, Tabitha separated herself from the group by going up on to the top deck, where she sunbathed, spreadeagled across two plastic chairs.

'Where are you from?' said an unfamiliar voice with a strong Indian accent. Opening one eye, the tigress squinted and sat half-upright. The man had a dark face, which made the whites of his eyes and his teeth stand out. Also, his tongue was bright pink.

'London,' said Tabitha.

'London, England?'

'Yes.'

'Would you like to be married?'

'Yes, but not to you.'

The man looked crestfallen. Tabitha imagined eloping with him and wondered what the group might think were she to do so. The scandal of it – *oooh la la*!

When they arrived on Elephant Island, there was a little Thomas the Tank Engine train that took them along the quay to a flight of steps hewn from the rock. They started to climb. Tabitha heard wheezing behind her and turned round.

'It's only my asthma,' said Gloria. 'Don't worry, you can go on ahead.'

Gloria was a nice, kind elephant whose new best friend the tigress wanted to be, so she slowed her pace. What new best friend wouldn't? she asked herself. To either side of the steps, there were stalls selling brightly coloured trinkets. The stalls were made from bamboo frames that were covered in white canvas that occasionally flapped in the breeze. Breathless, they reached the top. Andrew was standing on the far side of a crazily paved terrace at the entrance to some caves. There were large rock overhangs, which were oppressive and made Tabitha yearn for the Greek and Roman remains in the Mediterranean that she knew so well.

'The heaviness of the caves is designed to initiate a journey of inner transformation,' said Andrew from inside the first cave. His dulcet tones – which Tabitha had first noticed at Heathrow, when he'd said, 'Welcome on tour. I'm Andrew, your guide for the next three weeks' – drew her in. Still, she stood at the back of the group.

Andrew soon handed over to a local guide, whose hand and facial gestures mimicked those of the gods and goddesses whose stories she told. Tabitha was mesmerised and followed the local guide into the inner sanctum of the caves with the rest of the group. Here there was a lingam, or penis, coming out of a yoni, or vagina. How strange, thought Tabitha. It's usually doing the opposite. She also thought about how Hinduism could be reduced to a love of all things phallic. She didn't tell Andrew, of course. Instead, leaving the inner sanctum and then the other caves, she walked back across the crazily paved terrace, flanked by Andrew and Gloria. They were being watched by monkeys who sat on a low wall at the edge of the terrace, preening themselves.

'It's strange how familiarisation works,' said Tabitha.

'Go on,' said Andrew.

'Through a process that involves explanation and experience.' She could hear herself pontificating. Where only this morning she had been giggling at his local dress, now she was pontificating and hanging on his every word.

'How right you are,' he said.

Pleased as punch, Tabitha beamed.

On the ferry heading back to Mumbai, the sun was setting golden in a sky the colour of orange sherbet. Tabitha fell into conversation with the local guide, who was a fire-worshipping Parsi whose family had originally come from Gujarat.

'People in Mumbai expect me to be married and have children,' she said.

'So in Mumbai, so in London,' Tabitha agreed.

'They think we're the selfish ones not having children, but what about the planet? I think it's the other way around. They're the selfish ones.'

'I agree.'

Andrew was watching them. Tabitha imagined he was thinking about her. The easy way she fell into conversation with a woman her own age but from such another culture. She hoped that he was, and performed accordingly. Put another way, she flirted.

In the bar that night, the animals ate pasta with pesto, sitting on uncomfortable bamboo chairs arranged at low glass tables. Tabitha's back hurt. She put it down to Andrew's absence.

'Would you like a drink?' said Kathleen, flapping her wings.

'I'd love a dry white wine,' said Tabitha.

'Coming up.'

The wine arrived in two deeply cut, heavy crystal glasses. The tigress knocked hers back and the pelican kindly ordered her another. Then Kathleen got the bill.

'We won't be surviving on dry white wine on this tour,' she said.

Tabitha took it the wine was expensive, and thanked her.

CHAPTER 6

The next day, the tigress put her small green bag outside the door, ready for collection by the porters. She could get used to this life on tour, she thought. No more lugging of heavy rucksacks for her. It was a similar situation when they got to Mumbai's domestic airline terminal for their flight south to Calicut, because Andrew had managed to get them bumped up into first class. He was ever so proud. It was quite sweet really.

The first class cabin was at the front of the plane and they had it all to themselves. There were brown leather armchairs. Had the armchairs swivelled, Andrew and the animals might have thought they were in a James Bond movie. As it was, Andrew was sitting on the far side of the plane to Tabitha, beyond Rhonda, who was sitting next to Tabitha, and Geraldine, who was sitting next to Andrew. Andrew and Geraldine were deep in conversation – matters spiritual, Tabitha imagined. She wondered what it was about these animals – first the female bison, who had been deep in conversation with Andrew at passport control, and now the glang, mooing away. Then she realised it was her – Yours truly – who wanted to be deep in conversation with Andrew, finding out what made this man tick.

'Chicken or beef?' said the air hostess.

'Beef,' said Tabitha.

'I ordered vegetarian,' said Rhonda, rubbing her horn with her forefoot.

'It's on its way,' said the air hostess, putting down Tabitha's tray.

On top of her mound of beef casserole there was what looked like a green bean. The tigress popped it into her mouth. The heat was indescribable. She remembered a friend once telling her that the best thing to do, were she to mistake a chilli for a green bean, was to eat a banana. She didn't rate her chances of getting a banana on this particular flight, so she drank lots of water. This was the one thing her friend had told her not to do. Still, there was water in the plastic cup on her tray and water in the plastic bottle in the rucksack at her feet. She drank them both, then she asked Rhonda if she could have some of her water.

'If you must,' said Rhonda, again rubbing her horn with her forefoot.

'I must,' said Tabitha, flashing her claws. Eventually the heat in her mouth began to subside and, as the plane banked, she was able to appreciate the red-earthed Keralan landscape from the air.

Andrew and Tabitha walked across the tarmac together, the late afternoon sun on their backs. When they were outside the terminal in the shade, Andrew introduced the tigress to his assistant, who had flown in from Kashmir.

'Babaji, this is our reincarnated Sufi, who designs gardens,' he said. 'Nor Jahaan, this is Babaji,' he went on. Tabitha didn't know what 'Nor Jahaan' meant, just as she hadn't known what 'memsahib' meant, but she decided to take it as a term of endearment. Bowing her head as Babaji adorned her with a garland of giant marigolds, she felt like a queen.

'Namaste,' said Babaji, conjoining his hands in front of his chest and bowing. That was another new word on Tabitha, so she simply conjoined her paws, black velvet pads to die for, in front of her chest and bowed again.

Together with the other animals in the group, she then hopped aboard the twenty-seater bus that was to be their home for virtually the whole of the rest of the tour, and sat down one row from the back on the left-hand side. Tucking her tail in, she curled up and they set off, passing through tracts of green jungle and over brown languorous rivers by way of bridges that looked like they had been made from giant Meccano sets. They stopped for a cup of tea. Tabitha went to the loo and saw a big pile of tiny broken terracotta teacups. Recycling, Indian style, she thought.

On the way out, the hoolock said to her, 'It's all beyond the mind of man, isn't it?'

She thought it was a strange thing for a hoolock to say, so she said, 'Speak for yourself.'

The Mascot Beach Resort sat like a series of low-rise apartment blocks on top of a cliff. Tabitha was desperate to swim, so she went to the edge of the cliff and looked down. Dark blue waves were crashing on the rocks, creating white swirls of water, and there was a long, winding set of steps, hewn from the rock, that led down to the sea. The scene, lit by a watery sun, reminded her of a Hitchcock movie, so, shivering, she decided not to swim, and went with the other animals to check into the hotel. Then she went in search of a pool. She found one at the end of a concrete path, beyond a blue picket fence with a gate in it. Facilities permitting, she was planning to do fifty lengths every day of this tour. On this occasion, when she was halfway through, Gloria and Geraldine joined her. They both wore swimsuits with green and blue swirls, which reminded Tabitha of the ones her mother used to wear from Marks & Spencer. Geraldine also had on a yellow hat with rubber spikes that looked like a dandelion. While they were swimming up and down, waiters laid tables on the crazily paved terrace that surrounded the pool.

'Is there a party here tonight?' said Tabitha.

'Yes, memsahib,' said one of the waiters.

'Are we invited?'

'No, I'm afraid not. It's a private party to celebrate the eve of St Valentine's Day.'

Crestfallen, Tabitha returned to their room, meditated with Rhonda and decided to wear one of her favourite dresses for the evening. Dinner was set at a long, thin table on another crazily paved terrace lit by lookalike gas lamps. Once they were all seated, Andrew stood up and said that the rumours about the hotel were true: there was no alcohol, and nowhere nearby to buy alcohol. Eric, the male bison, and Callum, the male buffalo, made a right fuss. As only a male bison and a male buffalo would, thought Tabitha. Andrew sat down next to her. She sipped her lemon barley water demurely and thought how odd it was that the couples among them were the most consternated. It being the eve of St Valentine's Day, you would have thought that they'd be the happiest. Had she been in a couple, with Andrew for example, she would have been elated.

Clearing her throat, ready to make an announcement, she said, 'I think people who are different should be treated equally.'

'Is that because you're a Communist?' said Henry the hoolock.

'No,' she said.

'I believe in social hierarchy,' said Andrew.

The tigress was so shocked and disappointed in him that she nearly fell off her chair. First of all I nearly fall out of the taxi, now it's the chair. This is proving to be a dangerous holiday, she thought.

31

CHAPTER 7

At six o'clock the next morning a member of staff, who looked as tired as Tabitha felt, handed her a cup of cold black coffee and a stale biscuit.

'We were to have visited the Sri Muthappan temple yesterday evening, but our journey yesterday afternoon took longer than I anticipated, so we're going there this morning instead. I hope that's OK with everyone.'

Nothing we can do if it isn't, thought Tabitha, growling.

The approach to the Sri Muthappan temple was a covered walkway that looked like a cross between a Moroccan souk and an American shopping mall. At the entrance to the temple, there was a messy pile of shoes. Tabitha worried that her Merrells were going to get lost. All the same, she took them off and, having given them to the man in charge, stepped with her bare feet over the threshold of the temple. On the floor, there was a fine layer of mud. Her bare feet, black velvet pads to die for, slipped in it. For a moment she wanted to step back, then she thought, It's only slime, and proceeded anyway.

Inside, the light meter of her camera registered red. Too little light, she thought, as she headed for a large rectangular door on the far side of the temple. Outside, there was a set of stone steps down to a river. The sun rose red and the water was still, like burgundy glass. Tabitha descended the steps and turned to face the temple. Three saried women, babes on hips, were fast approaching, and she photographed them silhouetted against a grey sky. Then she returned to the interior, where she noticed that Henry, the male hoolock, was standing on the women's side of the temple. She thought about pointing it out to him but then she thought, What the hell, if the women are happy and he's happy, what does it matter if a hoolock stands on the wrong side of the temple?

All of a sudden two men – one dressed up as Vishnu the preserver, wearing an eagle headdress, and the other as Siva the transformer, silver almonds for eyes – started dancing. Their grass skirts gyrated and devotees pressed grubby brown notes into the hands of priests, wandering in among the crowds of devotees. Tabitha wondered why the devotees were pressing money into the hands of the priests, and resolved to ask Andrew. She thought it might have something to do with sex, because many of the women were so beautiful.

In a shrine to the left of the temple, Vishnu and Siva crossed swords. Tabitha hoped that they were going to proceed along the riverbank so that she could photograph them; but they didn't, so she couldn't.

At the entrance to the temple she was gratefully reunited with her shoes. Outside, she sat down on a step. Almost immediately a woman started shouting at her in a foreign language she didn't understand. The female bison helped her up. She hadn't expected the bison to be helpful, so she was pleasantly surprised. As immediately as she had started shouting, the woman stopped. Thank goodness for that, thought Tabitha.

'You were sitting on a step reserved for mothers giving babies their first rice,' said Tracey, the female bison.

'Oh,' said Tabitha.

'They use banana leaves as plates,' said Tracey.

'No wonder so many of the babies, with their sunken black eyes and sallow complexions, look so sick,' said the tigress.

'Have you noticed how clean the women's saris are even though their babies don't wear nappies?'

No I bloody haven't, Tabitha wanted to growl. Instead, following Andrew's lead when he was talking to the pelican in the taxi from the airport, she kept calm. To be honest, she wanted to phone the UN and tell them about the babies; but she didn't think it would be worth it, because she didn't think they'd take any notice of little old her.

Back at the hotel, before leaving for the River Retreat Hotel on the banks of the River Bharatapuzha, Tabitha drank another cup of cold black coffee and ate a rubbery omelette flecked with red and green peppers. In her room, she wrestled with the traveller's age-old problem: bulky winter clothes worn to the airport take up more room than neatly packed summer clothes. What to do with the bulky winter clothes? That was the question. In this instance the answer was to stuff bulky clothes into a white plastic bag found in the corner of the room.

Gloria was having a nap on the back seat of the bus. Tabitha stuffed her luggage, normally stowed on the back seat, to either side of the elephant, and took up her regular seat one row from the back on the left-hand side. Tucking her tail in, she curled up. The bus set off. Almost immediately and without explanation, Gloria shot past Tabitha and there was an enormous pile of what looked like crushed Pringles on the floor – a purple shag pile carpet.

'Thank goodness it wasn't me,' said Tracey. Only thinking about herself, growled Tabitha, noting the fact in her imaginary little black book.

'Nor me,' said Kathleen, flicking what looked like a bit of crushed Pringle off her white feathered shoulder pad. Self centred pelican, growled Tabitha, also noting the fact in that imaginary little black book of hers. She looked out of the window. Gloria was retching into the ditch. Now she got it; the elephant was being sick. Tabitha wanted to help her new best friend but she was stuck in the bus, so she continued to watch. Geraldine the glang laid down her copy of the *Hindi Times* to absorb the sick in the bus and Andrew waited – patiently, thought Tabitha – for Gloria to recover. When the elephant did eventually get back on the bus she sat at the front, so some animals, but not Tabitha, had to move round. There was a terrible crackle as Babaji turned on the microphone, then Andrew's voice boomed out:

'I think we could all do with a chai stop,' he said, 'so I've asked the driver to take us to the nearest cafe.'

In the cafe, Andrew sat to Tabitha's left and Henry to her right.

'What did you think of the performance in the temple this morning?' said Andrew.

Tabitha wanted to tell Andrew that she had other things on her mind, such as Gloria's well-being, but she didn't dare. To be honest, she was intimidated by Andrew. Not that she admitted it then.

'Ritual of the kind we saw in the temple is designed to foster social cohesion in traditional Indian societies,' he went on.

As an anthropologist, Tabitha wanted to ask him what he meant by 'traditional'. Also, she wanted to ask him about the impact of such ritual on women and children, but again she didn't dare. It was odd, really, a tigress being intimidated by a man, but there it was.

'I'm not sure that such ritual will go very far towards finding replacement partners for abandoned women,' said Henry, pretty much apropos of nothing. 'Wouldn't it be better to introduce marriage guidance into India?' he went on.

'Hmmm,' said Andrew.

Back on the bus, the driver had jettisoned the purple shag pile carpet and had a clothes peg on his nose.

'Time for some lunch,' said Andrew. They drove to another cafe. There wasn't a single table big enough to accommodate the whole group, so Geraldine, Gloria, Henry, Leticia, Babaji and Andrew were allocated to one table while Rhonda, Kathleen, Eric, Tracey, Callum and Clodagh were allocated to another. Tracey went to the bathroom to powder her bison's nose. When she came back and saw the group that had been allocated to her table, she looked as if she'd been snubbed. Tabitha would have said it was because Tracey thought that Andrew had allocated Tracey to what he considered to be the lower-class table.

'Let's play a game,' said Henry, addressing the upper-class table. 'Everyone look at the wall opposite, then with your eyes shut point at yourself. What do you see?' Nobody said a thing. 'Seeing an amorphous grey mass indicates connectedness to the material world.' As nobody saw an amorphous grey mass on the upper-class table, they must all, by implication, be connected to the spiritual world, thought Tabitha.

Like a puppy dog, Andrew followed her out of the cafe.

'What did you see?' he said.

'Nothing in particular,' she said, mumbling. In truth she recalled an occasion when she had gone to see an acupuncturist. When she was coming round from a faint, she had seen a woman in black sitting in the corner of the room. She was talking to Tabitha, but Tabitha couldn't hear what she was saying.

Back on the bus, Andrew said he was going to administer another of his sleeping pills, by which he meant one of his long talks. This time it was about the temple visit of that morning.

'The silver almonds that were stuck over Siva's eyes have two purposes. The first is to represent his sightlessness and the second is to reflect the image of the devoted onlooker.'

On he droned. Tabitha fell asleep. When she woke up, she had come to an understanding. Men like Andrew, with degrees in

English literature from Cambridge (which Andrew had let slip that he had) and a love of all things Indian, will never appreciate the impact of ritual on vulnerable groups such as women and children. Even if someone like Tabitha did manage to pluck up the courage to speak with Andrew, there would be no point in trying to enlighten him. He was stuck in his ways. A bombshell was needed.

His next announcement related to the River Retreat Hotel on the banks of the River Bharatapuzha.

'It's where we'll be staying tonight.' he said. 'It was once a palace belonging to the Maharaj of Cochin.'

Sounds even grander than the places we've been staying in so far, thought Tabitha.

'We've been given a room with a small double bed,' said Geraldine. Tabitha imagined the elephant in bed with the glang and smiled.

'I'll see what I can do,' said the receptionist. Once she had sorted a suitable room for Geraldine and Gloria, and the porter had taken Tabitha's small green bag up to her room, Tabitha went for a walk. To be honest, she had a feeling as though she couldn't wait to get away from the group.

A wire fence surrounded the hotel grounds. On the side of the hotel that formed the riverbank there was a small set of steps, hewn from the turf. The risers were mud. By crawling under the wire fence, Tabitha could descend the steps. At the bottom, she jumped down onto the riverbed. Although it was technically dry, there were long, twisting gravel tongues sprouting willow herb and grass that separated shallow pools of water. To her right there was an enormous rusted red viaduct that looked like it had been made from that giant Meccano set. Must be a huge river when it's in full flow, she thought.

Tabitha made her way along one of the twisting gravel tongues until she came to a pool. In the next-door pool were two fathers playing with their children, and Tabitha realised how much she envied them their family life. She toyed with the idea of going for a swim. Unfortunately, she had neither her swimsuit nor her mosquito repellent, so that was a bit of a non-starter. Also, she thought about going for a walk across the riverbed and returning by way of the rusted red viaduct, but although she liked circuitous routes, she wasn't brave enough. Then, suddenly and strangely, she was gripped by a strong desire to be back with the group.

Tabitha paid Gloria and Geraldine a visit.

'How are you?' she said.

'I'm afraid we're both feeling rather unwell,' said Geraldine. 'Gloria is still feeling sick and despite being a doctor, albeit one with a speciality in psychosexual medicine, I've managed to take an antibiotic on an empty stomach.'

'Oh dear,' said Tabitha. 'I am sorry.'

'Neither of us will be joining you for dinner, I'm afraid, so please do send our apologies to Andrew.'

The thought of having to have supper without either Geraldine or Gloria filled Tabitha with dread. Still, she changed into her green and white dress with its Jackpot label on the outside and descended the long, sloping lawn immediately outside the hotel, where a white plastic table and chairs had been set up.

Luckily, dinner wasn't as frightening as she imagined it was going to be. Afterwards, when the hoolocks had excused themselves – to read their spiritual tomes, so they said – Andrew came to sit next to her. Tabitha's heart beat like the clappers.

'In my life,' he said, 'meditation is a means of transcendence.'

Tabitha couldn't think what to say, then all of a sudden she said, 'In my life, immanence is of equal importance.' She was quite pleased with herself.

Then Andrew said, 'Did you know that the leader of your meditation society failed to complete his training?'

If the leader of her meditation society failed to complete his training then her meditation must be crap, she thought. Tabitha was shocked to the very core of her being.

'No,' she said.

Andrew withdrew. Dropped a bombshell of his own, then withdrew, just like that.

'You look like you could do with a beer,' said Eric, taking his place.

'Yes please,' said Tabitha, even though she didn't really like beer.

When he returned with two beers, Eric went on, 'The hoolocks have been arguing on account of the attention he's been paying you.'

'How do you know?'

'Their door was ajar and my wife heard them.'

'Did she now?'

'You look like you could do with another beer.'

'Well, if you insist,' said Tabitha. The first beer had gone straight to her head; the second beer made her feel really quite drunk. Added to which, she felt surrounded by Andrew's meditators; the rhino, the pelican, the bison and the buffalo were all still up and about. Her meditators – the elephant, the glang and the hoolocks – had all taken to their beds for one reason or another. What was she to do? Stick with her meditators or become one of Andrew's meditators? That was the question now. Were she a lone wolf, she would have howled into the darkness, 'What am I to do? What am I to do?'

CHAPTER 8

What with dreaming about Leticia and Tracey chasing her round the mulberry bush and having to fix the air conditioning unit above Rhonda's head without waking her, Tabitha had had a busy night. Not much shut-eye was beginning to take its toll. After breakfast – a cup of strong black coffee and a rubbery omelette – she managed, by virtue of some careful rearrangement, to jettison the white plastic bag.

'Off we go,' said Babaji, boarding the bus.

This morning, much to Tabitha's relief, no one was sick, and they soon arrived at the Kerala Kalamandalam, a centre for the performing arts. A tour had been organised for them by the management, so Andrew was able to hand over the reins. Tabitha stood at the back and noticed that the shape of the dancers' hand and feet gestures mimicked the roofline of the building. It was like at the caves on Elephant Island, where she'd noticed that the gestures of the guide mimicked those of the gods and goddesses whose stories she told. Anything for a good connection, she thought. Ever the anthropologist, she mused.

Tabitha went outside to take a photo of the roofline.

All of a sudden, a woman started shouting at her in a foreign language she didn't understand. Hurrying towards the bus, she hopped aboard and kept a low profile. The woman started shouting at Andrew in English. From her position hidden low inside the bus, Tabitha could lip-read the woman.

'Photography is not allowed,' she was shouting. Tabitha hoped that Andrew was defending her to the hilt, but feared not. More like he was wishing he didn't have such a reprobate for a group member.

The bus set off. Tabitha looked out through the back window. The big entrance gates were electric. The woman was standing just inside them, waving her fist. If she thought Tabitha was coming back any time soon, she should think again.

At the ordinary elephant sanctuary where they arrived next, the ordinary elephants' chapped and bleeding legs were chained to telegraph poles, and the thought of their pain made Tabitha wince. What it must have been like for Gloria, being an elephant herself, Tabitha dreaded to think.

'Are these elephants ever allowed out?' she said.

'Once a year during the monsoon season to mate,' said the mahout.

In the distance, Tabitha could see an ordinary elephant lying on its side with what looked like a hosepipe over it. She thought it was about to enjoy its ablutions, so she went over to photograph it. In fact, the elephant had had one of its tusks removed. A big wad of cotton wool had been used to stem the flow of blood, filling the gap where the tusk had been.

'This elephant must have had an infection,' said Tabitha to Geraldine.

'Yes,' said Geraldine. The ordinary elephant was lying at the foot of the mahout. Something about its body lying vulnerable at the foot of a man, however well-meaning the man, perturbed Tabitha.

On the other side of the sanctuary she could see another ordinary elephant eating bamboo and rubbing its behind against the coconut palm to which it was chained. Tabitha took one photo, then another.

Onlookers gathered.

'Watch out,' they shouted.

What Tabitha hadn't realised was that, in spite of the ordinary elephant's chain, she was within range of the ordinary elephant. She took a step back, out of range of the ordinary elephant. All of a sudden, the ordinary elephant stopped dead in its tracks, and it started raining coconuts. The onlookers laughed.

Tabitha sighed with relief.

Babaji appeared. 'The temple we were planning to visit before lunch is about to close. Unless we go now, we won't make it,' he said.

As they walked towards the temple, Andrew was at Tabitha's side.

'The approach to the temple is similar to the temple we visited yesterday,' she said.

'How observant you are, my dear Nor Jahaan. Have you noticed that the banners overhead are like a rainbow?'

'Except that the colours are in the wrong order,' she said.

'Pedant,' said Andrew jokingly.

Unfortunately, the temple was shut.

'We'll meet in the restaurant on the other side of the road at one o'clock. Until then, you can have some free time,' Andrew told the group.

That's the first free time we will have had since we started the tour, thought Tabitha. Time for some shopping, she decided. She imagined the stallholders were going to be all over the animals like a rash, but in fact they were remarkably reserved, which was most refreshing.

*

42

Tabitha was the first to arrive at the restaurant. Must be the Andrew effect again, she thought, working its on-timely magic. But, because she was hardly ever early for anything, she found it unnerving.

Babaji was sitting on a beige suede banquette, running his hands through his curly dark locks. 'Come and sit here,' he said, patting the banquette beside him.

Tabitha did as she was told. There was an awkward silence. She chose her words carefully. She didn't want Babaji thinking she thought he was an interloper who had abandoned his own country in favour of an easier economic life in India. From research that she'd done, she knew that people didn't abandon their homes lightly.

'Are your family originally from Kashmir?' she said.

'The media always gives an inaccurate picture of Kashmir. In truth, it's a heavenly place,' he said.

'I'm sure,' she said, before asking Babaji how he found his work with Andrew.

'If it wasn't for Andrew restraining me, I'd have you all on leads,' he said.

She laughed. Then Andrew and the other animals came into the restaurant.

'So this is where you two have been hiding,' said Andrew.

'Just chatting,' said Babaji nonchalantly.

To accommodate Andrew between Babaji and herself, Tabitha shuffled her bottom along the banquette.

'I take it you're joining us,' she said.

'Of course,' he said, sitting down between Babaji and Tabitha. As only an alpha male would, she thought. 'And so are the others,' he went on.

'As planned,' she said, mimicking Andrew.

Andrew arched an eyebrow. 'As planned,' he said.

While they were eating their food, there was another awkward silence.

'There's a school in Kensington,' said Tabitha, 'that prides itself on educating children from a wide variety of cultural backgrounds. Also, it teaches Sanskrit and meditation.'

'I went to a convent,' said Kathleen.

'We sent our boys there,' said Henry.

For a moment, Tabitha thought the male hoolock had sent his boys to a convent, then she realised her mistake.

'One of them liked it, the other didn't,' he continued.

Andrew, who had momentarily left the proceedings, returned. 'I've just found out there's going to be an elephant procession in one of the nearby villages,' he said.

If anybody other than Andrew had interrupted Tabitha for what would have been the third time, she would have blown a gasket. Lucky it was Andrew.

Andrew and the animals walked along a high-sided track cut deep into the floor of the Keralan woods. Families, many of whom had put oil lamps out in front of their homes, lined the track. There was a cacophony of noise, especially from a merry band of drummers who were accompanying the procession.

The elephants started coming out of the jungle. Each one had a mayoral chain around its neck and a headdress covered in coloured baubles. On the back of each elephant there was a group of five or six crouching mahouts.

Tabitha jumped up on to the side of the track and took photos. Then, when the procession had passed by, she joined in at the back.

'Where are you from?' said a fellow member of the procession.

'London,' she said.

'London, England?'

'Yes.'

As the procession surged forward and the track became a road lined with turkey oaks, the tigress continued to take photos.

The procession followed the road, turned to the right and reached its final destination, a clearing in the woods at a crossroads. Tabitha continued to take photos. Elephants and their mahouts assembled. They erected placards, opened parasols, displayed decorated plates and waved feathered fans. The drumming got louder. Just as it reached its climax, the film in her camera ran out. She struggled to reload her camera as fast as she could. Again the crowd surged forward, taking her with it. All of a sudden, she was right at the centre of the clearing in the trees at the crossroads and she was surrounded by five frenzied dancers, a fertility goddess and four demons, all of whom were crazily whirling, twirling and swirling.

Tabitha scoured the crowd for Andrew. She wanted to thank him for giving her such a wonderful photographic opportunity, the best she'd ever had. Unfortunately, she couldn't see him or any of the other members of their party anywhere. Put another way, she was lost. She tried not to panic. A group of men surrounded her, and they appeared to know where she had come from and, more importantly, where she was going. This supported one of her pet anthropological theories: people in small-scale communities spend an inordinate amount of time watching the comings and goings of newcomers.

'Tabitha,' she heard Andrew calling. Turning round, she realised that the bus was right there behind her and that Andrew was calling from the door.

'I thought I was lost,' she said.

Two hours later, it was time for another chai stop. The shack was similar to one where they had stopped before. Part of a chain, thought Tabitha.

'Can you help me?' said Kathleen to Babaji.

'If I can,' said Babaji.

'That man over there just tried to diddle me.'

'By how much?'

'Three rupees.'

Babaji and Tabitha couldn't believe their ears. They looked at each other.

All of a sudden, Henry started shouting. 'He's saying I only paid for one tea, when in fact I paid for two.'

Another of Tabitha's pet anthropological theories: animals deprived of their creature comforts have a tendency to lose perspective. One day, she resolved, she would try to get her pet theories published in *Anthropology Today*. Also, she resolved to try not to lose her perspective.

A sound came to her ears: 'Om, sizzle, om, sizzle, om, sizzle.' The 'om' reminded her of her meditative practice. As for the 'sizzle', she hadn't a clue. She headed off in the direction of the marquee from which the sound appeared to be emanating, and peered in. Hundreds of devotees were sitting cross-legged in rows on the floor. In front of them, a priest with a loudhailer was leading a mass chant.

'Om,' went the priest.

'Om,' went the devotees. At the same time they threw handfuls of rice into small metal bowls of boiling oil in front of them. 'Sizzle,' went the rice. Tabitha entered the marquee, sat down at the back and started to chant. She was just getting going when Andrew tapped her on the shoulder.

'I'm afraid we need to head off,' he said.

The bus drove in through a gap in the curved walls of the five-star Brunton Boatyard Hotel and came to a stop outside the door. They descended from the bus and walked across the well-raked pea gravel. Once inside, they were ushered into a well-polished wooden-panelled lobby and garlanded with flowers. A waiter bearing a silver platter arrived and used tongs to extract warm, wet flannels from their plastic wrappers. He gave them to the animals. Tabitha wiped her paws, black velvet pads to die for, as well as her face. Another waiter arrived bearing orange fruit cocktails on a silver platter. The first waiter took away her wet flannel and offered her a seat. She sipped her fruit cocktail. When she'd finished the liquid, she pierced the fruit segments with a cocktail stick, sucked them dry, ate them, then ate the ice too. An overhead fan whirred above. It was like a propeller and was controlled by a series of pulleys and ropes. Two porters appeared. One was carrying Tabitha's small green bag. The other was carrying Rhonda's two enormous suitcases.

All together, they set off for their room, which was on the ground floor. When the porter opened the door, Tabitha took a sharp intake of breath. The room had two enormous beds, large wooden headboards, blue and white striped bed linen, a fully functioning air conditioning unit and French windows opening out on to a herringbone brick terrace, which was edged with box. In front of them lay a view of the sea.

Rhonda stayed out on the terrace. Tabitha went back into their room. There was a knock at the door.

'Room service,' said the waiter, who was carrying a tray.

'I don't recall placing an order,' said Tabitha.

'Room 101,' said the waiter.

Tabitha looked at the room number on the door and back at the waiter, then she took the tray. She carried it out on to the terrace. Rhonda was reclining on a deckchair and stroking her horn with her forefoot.

'Here,' said Tabitha, putting the tray down with the slightest of reproachful thuds. Rhonda, of course, didn't say a thing, not so much as a 'thank you', never mind a 'sorry, I forgot to tell you I ordered room service'. She didn't even offer Tabitha a cup of tea, but just carried on stroking her horn with her forefoot and drinking her tea.

It was time for a swim. Grabbing a towel from the bathroom, Tabitha changed into her highly fashionable but non-matching bikini and headed for the pool. The signs to the pool were hand-painted. It was getting dark when she got there and descended backwards into the pool by way of a ladder. As she swam breaststroke up and down, the water was warm and she looked up. A marbled moon hung pale in a red-edged tropical sky.

Geraldine joined her. 'Dinner's at eight,' she said.

I know that, thought Tabitha, growling to herself. Even so, she was late for dinner. All of the group were present. There weren't enough chairs.

'Here, have mine,' said Henry, getting another chair for himself.

Eric, who was on the far side of the table, winked at Tabitha. Tracey, his wife, stared daggers.

Tabitha winked back at Eric. 'How kind,' she said. Henry's chair was still warm. When he sat down, his thigh was touching hers. Andrew and Leticia, Henry's wife, were deep in conversation and didn't seem to notice any of this.

'We don't exist,' said Henry.

'Too true,' said Geraldine.

Tabitha wasn't in the mood for philosophising with a non-existent hoolock, let alone a non-existent glang, so she ate her dinner, took to her bed and fantasised about Andrew. Talk about erotic.

CHAPTER 9

For the first time since being 'on tour', Tabitha had had a good night's sleep, and managed to swim fifty lengths of the pool with no problem. She put on her favourite white T-shirt over a pale blue linen pencil skirt cut on the bias, and felt she was looking good as she sipped her coffee and ate mango from a fruit platter.

'The bus is leaving at nine. We had better get going,' said Gloria.

Tabitha found herself scurrying across a terracotta-tiled court-yard somewhere at the centre of the hotel. The heels of her pointed black suede slip-ons went clickety-clack on the terracotta tiles like a stag's hooves on stone. At the centre of the courtyard there was a sweet-smelling frangipani tree. She breathed in the scent and listened. Quietly at first, the sound of a man's softly cushioned shoe soles emerged. Then the sound got louder. Then silence.

'There's no need to look so concerned, my Nor Jahaan. There's been a delay and the bus isn't leaving until nine thirty,' said Andrew.

Tabitha loved it when Andrew called her his Nor Jahaan, even though she still didn't know what it meant. Her heart skipped a beat.

She went back to the room. Rhonda was gathering her things together.

'Are you looking forward to our trip to the Mattancherry Palace today?' she said. Tabitha was gobsmacked that Rhonda was talking to her. She knew that their visit to the Mattancherry Palace wasn't until the following day. She was just about to remind Rhonda when Rhonda said, 'That's not until tomorrow.'

Too right, thought Tabitha. And you know what? Talking to yourself – first sign of madness.

The hotel boutique was to the right of the hotel entrance. With time to spare, Tabitha decided to pay it a visit. Kathleen was also in the shop. Tabitha caught sight of some denim embroidered with white flowers. From the packed rails she pulled it out. It was a nice shirt, she thought.

'That's a nice top,' said Kathleen. And, thought Tabitha, you're not going to get your wings on it. Tabitha clasped the top to her small but perfectly formed breasts, then she paid for it and put it on over her white T-shirt.

She made her way down the aisle of the bus.

'That's a nice top,' said Tracey.

'Thank you,' said Tabitha. 'It was only a pound.'

'The blue complements your eyes.'

Andrew and the animals wandered down the beach to the water's edge.

'These huge see-sawlike structures, made from bamboo, nets at one end, stones at the other, are known locally as Chinese fishermen's nets,' said Andrew.

Tabitha had first seen them photographed against a blood-red sky on the front cover of the *Financial Times* magazine *How to Spend It*. Photographing them against a grey sky at ten o'clock of a morning in India wasn't quite the same thing.

'Come and see,' said one of the fishermen. He showed her his catch, a writhing mass of sardines, which shimmered silver, pink and green.

Walking back up the beach, Tabitha could see the others, who were examining white cotton clothes at a stall shaded by a huge umbrella. Tracey blocked her path.

'It's preposterous,' she said.

'What?' said Tabitha wearily.

'At one pound fifty, Clodagh thought that these fans were too expensive, so she won't buy one.'

While Tabitha respected Tracey's right to express herself, she wasn't so keen on being bullied into supporting her views. Keeping quiet, she relished the power of silence. Eventually, Tracey flounced off. Touché, thought Tabitha. She didn't much take to Tracey.

They walked along the beach past a fort and came to a track heading inland. To either side of the track, there were walls covered with peeling white paint and creepers.

On the road, on the far side under a tree, there was a snake charmer sitting cross-legged on the ground. In front of him, also on the ground, were two baskets, one with a lid, the other without. Tabitha put a crumpled brown note into the basket without a lid and waited. The snake charmer took off the lid of the other basket and started to play. The slithery black cobras began to uncoil, then raised their heads and spat with their forked tongues.

Frightened, as any tigress would be, Tabitha hid behind her camera, took photos and moved swiftly on.

'You haven't paid,' said the snake charmer.

'Yes I have,' she said firmly.

They arrived in front of an Anglican church. Andrew gathered the animals together.

'As I said yesterday,' he said, 'I'm not trying to convert you to Hinduism, just trying to demonstrate the Keralan ability to live together irrespective of difference. Here's an Anglican church, and in due course I'll be showing you a Catholic cathedral and a Jewish synagogue.'

Inside the Anglican church, Tabitha sat in a pew next to Gloria.

A vicar was their guide. 'Vasco da Gama was buried in Cochin before being exhumed and returned to Portugal for reburial,' he said.

The walls and the vaulted ceilings of the church were painted pale yellow and there was a lot of dark brown wood. Overhead, large fans whirred.

'It's all very austere,' said Gloria.

'I need to pee,' said Tabitha, excusing herself.

The only thing was, she couldn't find a loo. Circumnavigating the church, she looked for a place to pee. All the windows in between the buttresses of the church came down to the ground except one. Accordingly, she squatted. It wasn't long before a small river ran beyond the buttresses and across the path. Lucky the bishop isn't coming along the path, she thought, sighing with relief in more ways than one.

Their group was crossing a patch of open ground in front of the church. A salesman had been selling toys to Geraldine and Clodagh outside the church. All of a sudden, the salesman gave chase.

'You haven't paid,' he shouted.

Geraldine clasped her toy cobra to her ample bosom. 'Yes I have,' she said.

'No you haven't,' shouted the salesman.

Tabitha thought about intervening. Had she done so, she would have pointed out that Geraldine's salary was the greater of the two.

Geraldine gave the toy cobra back to the salesman. He threw it on the ground. Geraldine picked it up. Clodagh comforted her. What a nice buffalo, thought Tabitha.

*

52

The Catholic cathedral was bright yellow on the outside, with two white towers that looked like meringues. Inside, the stained-glass saints were lit up and the tiles were highly patterned. Andrew came over to Tabitha. Her heart beat faster.

'Do you know the fourteen Stations of the Cross?' he said.

'I wish I did, but I don't,' she said.

Andrew wandered off. Tabitha wished that he wouldn't just wander off like that. Why? Because she would have liked to tell him that she was beginning to understand his love of all things Indian and, more importantly, to share it.

The bus appeared. They hopped on, and the bus wove its way through the tiny backstreets of Cochin until they arrived at a car park just outside the Jewish quarter and disembarked into a market selling all sorts of knick-knacks, from stuffed elephants to Rajisthani puppets.

'The synagogue will shut at twelve and you need to be back at the bus for one, so I suggest you visit the synagogue first before indulging your shopaholic tendencies,' said Andrew.

Does he think we're stupid or something? Tabitha wondered. They hurried to the synagogue, which was a white building with a dome. Inside, Tabitha took photos of the panelled ceiling and the coloured glass chandeliers, then left quickly to indulge her shopaholic tendencies.

'Where are you going now?' said Gloria.

'Back to look at some puppets I saw on the way here,' said Tabitha.

She could only find a queen puppet with an evil face and a king puppet with a kindly face. She bought them all the same, then she went for a wander, which was interrupted by Gloria.

'I want to know what you think of these jackets,' she said, making Tabitha jump. 'I am sorry,' she went on. 'I didn't mean to frighten you. I just wanted to buy one of these jackets for Hermione and I wanted to know what you thought of them.'

'They're too loud,' said Tabitha.

Gloria looked at the price tag. 'Too expensive too,' she said, waving her trunk.

'Why don't we go next door?' said Tabitha.

Next door there was a similar jacket but in a subtler colour.

'Try it on,' said Gloria. 'Do a twirl.'

Tabitha did so.

'That's perfect. What good taste you have.'

While Gloria was paying for her purchase, Tabitha looked through a pile of Moghul prints that were sitting on the counter. She guessed the most expensive and got it right every time. Luckily for her bank account, she didn't like any of them. Gloria looked at her watch.

'Five past one,' she said.

'We had better run,' said Tabitha.

'It's all very well for you,' said Gloria, 'but I've got all these bags.'

'What have you been buying?'

'Curtain fabric for the new house, a waistcoat for my husband, a sari for my daughter – I could go on.'

'Tell me later. For now we need to get going.'

'What's our excuse for being late?'

'You had a relapse.'

By the time they got to the bus, Gloria was huffing and puffing like a steam train. Andrew was frowning. He doesn't look like he's best pleased, thought Tabitha. Hopping aboard the bus, they made their way down the aisle. The bison held their heads in the air. The hoolocks and the buffalo stared out the window. Rhonda and Kathleen stared at them. By the time Tabitha and Gloria got to the back seat, they could contain themselves no longer. Collapsing in fits of giggles, they rolled around like naughty schoolgirls.

*

54

At lunchtime, back at the hotel, Tabitha wandered into the dining room and found Andrew.

'Rhonda has asked me to tell you she's feeling unwell and she won't be joining us for lunch,' she said to him.

'Thank you for letting me know,' he said.

Tabitha was sitting to Andrew's right. Leticia was to his left. He turned to her. Tabitha listened to the music.

Some time later Geraldine said, 'It's the Queen of Sheba.'

Tabitha was surprised by the length of time it took Geraldine to say it because the glang, she happened to know, was very musical. Tabitha hadn't so much as a musical bone in her body. She looked at her watch. It was ten to two.

'I had better go,' she said.

'Where are you off to?' said Geraldine.

'I'm going to have an Ayurvedic massage,' said Tabitha.

'Don't be late. I'm after you,' said Geraldine.

In preparation for her Ayurvedic massage, Tabitha had put on her 'just in case' bra. The Ayurvedic centre was to the right of the hotel entrance. She arrived on time.

'If you'd like to go through,' said the receptionist, 'you can undress and relax. The masseuse will be along shortly.'

Tabitha had never been in an Ayurvedic treatment room before. In the middle there was a stone slab supported on two pillars and covered in blue plastic. She took her clothes off down to her bra and underpants and lay on the plastic-covered stone slab. Try as she might, she couldn't relax on the plastic.

At ten past two the masseuse, a dark-skinned elderly woman, thickset and knee-high to a grasshopper, came into the room. Her idea of 'on time' and Tabitha's were obviously different. So were their ideas of 'undressed'.

'You can take off your bra and underpants,' said the masseuse.

Tabitha did so and stood naked to one side of the plastic-covered stone slab. The masseuse tied a string around her middle, shot her hands between her thighs and grabbed a small rectangular piece of paper. As a result, Tabitha had a piece of paper – a bit like a sanitary towel – between her thighs.

'You can lie down now,' said the masseuse, pouring oil from one hand to the other and dolloping it onto Tabitha's fur. She rubbed it in.

'Relax,' she said.

It's all very well saying relax, but when you're lying on a plastic slab covered in oil and trying not to slip off, thought Tabitha, it's nigh on impossible.

'Kikkhi?' said the masseuse.

'That's right,' said Tabitha. She'd chosen kikkhi from a long list of possibilities. According to the blurb in the leaflet, it was good for her shoulder, and boy, was her shoulder hurting.

The masseuse picked up a small muslin bag filled with kikkhi and rubbed it into Tabitha's shoulder just as hard as she could.

'Better?' she said.

'Not really,' said Tabitha.

'How long have you had the pain?'

'A couple of years, on and off.'

'Come back tomorrow.'

'I can't. We're leaving.'

'Then you'll just have to get in the shower.'

Thank goodness for that, thought Tabitha. To be honest, she couldn't wait to remove the oil from her fur. Slithering off the plastic-covered slab, she got into the shower. The masseuse handed her a jug containing a mixture that looked like guacamole.

'Here, try this,' said the masseuse. 'It'll leave your fur feeling soft as a baby's bottom.'

In the reception area, Geraldine, the doctor with the speciality in psychosexual medicine, was sitting on a wooden-slatted bench swinging her legs.

'How was it?' she said.

Tabitha didn't want to put Geraldine off, so she said it was interesting. She couldn't wait to swim. The water was milky turquoise. As she swam up and down, she felt like Cleopatra. Afterwards, she spread a blue and white striped towel over a yellow and white striped sun lounger, applied what she considered to be the appropriate amount of Ambre Solaire and joined the rhino, the pelican, the hoolocks, the bison and the buffalo, who were in various states of recline.

She was dying to tell the other animals all about her Ayurvedic massage. If nothing else, she thought, I want to come to terms with the experience. She started, but nobody seemed to be listening, so she stopped.

Geraldine appeared and was totally calm, as if she had actually enjoyed the massage.

Tabitha wondered if Geraldine's experience as a doctor of psychosexual medicine had prepared her for being naked and covered in oil on a slithering piece of blue plastic and then slathered in a guacamole-like substance in the shower. Or was it just yours truly being silly and immature?

In the early evening, they went to the Cochin Community Centre, where they watched three male actors, one of whom drummed and two of whom danced, demonstrating a range of hand and facial gestures, which represented emotions that were to be used in a play. The play followed and was about a man responding to a woman's declaration of love. At first he responded positively, then he changed his mind and murdered her. Heaving, Gloria began to cry, big soulful elephant tears, and Tabitha comforted her.

They had dinner at the Brunton Boatyard Hotel, and afterwards Andrew, Babaji, Gloria and Tabitha enjoyed themselves in the upstairs dining room over a drink. Everybody else had taken to their beds.

'What did you think of the play?' said Andrew.

'What did it actually mean?' said Tabitha.

'Think of India as a series of multi-dimensional Venn diagrams, then let it wash all over you,' he said.

'I'll try,' said Tabitha hopefully.

'How's it all going?' said Gloria.

'To tell the truth,' said Andrew, 'we've been having rather a difficult time of it, haven't we, Babaji?'

'Staving off the Italian hordes,' said Babaji.

'What he means,' said Andrew, 'is that the hotel was overbooked and we had difficulty getting you all in.'

When Andrew and Babaji turned in, Tabitha said to Gloria, 'Time for one last dip?'

'That would be lovely,' she said.

It was a hot and sticky night and they swam up and down in the refreshingly cool water.

'This being "on tour" is beginning to feel less like one continuous cocktail party, a little less surreal, I'd say,' said Gloria.

Speak for yourself, thought Tabitha. She felt buffeted by Andrew. One minute he was calling her his Nor Jahaan, the next minute he was cool and distant. She didn't know where she stood, and desperately wanted to know how he felt about her.

CHAPTER 10

It was early, first light, and Tabitha couldn't sleep. Quiet as a church mouse, as she didn't want to wake Rhonda, she crept out of bed (difficult for a tigress), grabbed her diary and went into the bathroom. Installed on the loo, she wrote her diary. Then it was back to bed for some more shut-eye before she woke up, carried out her ablutions, swam, meditated, and ate her breakfast.

On the back seat of the bus there was a cooler full of water bottles. Taking one, Tabitha downed her nutritional supplements and felt ready for the day ahead.

The murals at the Mattancherry Palace were exquisite – quite the most delicate things she'd ever seen. The only thing was – guess what? – she needed to pee. She couldn't find a loo. She could find a yellow bucket in the administrative quarters of the building. But she couldn't find a drain. Nothing she could do but leave the bucket half-full and hope that nobody mistook it for water.

At lunch, back at the hotel, Rhonda announced, apropos of nothing, that Andrew had a girlfriend. Recalling the conversation in the taxi from the airport, when Andrew had definitely said he was single, Tabitha did a double take.

After lunch there was a period of free time. In the lobby Tabitha found a writing desk where, with pen and postcard, she installed herself.

'*Dear Stevenavitch,*' she wrote. '*I miss you so much, especially your humour. I am desperate to escape the confines of the group. In particular, I want to explore the real India beyond the walls of the luxury hotels we have been staying in. Not that I've got a problem with luxury, as you know. I love it – just not all of the time. As you would say, it is only through the appreciation of opposites that we come to understand the whole. Love, Tabitha.*'

Popping the postcard in the box at the end of the reception desk, Tabitha crossed herself and prayed for its safe delivery.

The bus drew out of the hotel grounds. Tabitha said goodbye to her favourite hotel of the tour so far, then she looked out of the window.

'We're now passing through the coir-producing heartland of Aleppey,' said Andrew.

His sleeping pill, together with the movement of the bus, soon induced a stupor and the tigress fell deeply asleep. When she awoke, it was late afternoon. The bus was just pulling up at the side of a canal. The heat was thick, and all was quiet on the canal's palm-fringed banks.

'The canal is part of a network of waterways known locally as the Kerala backwaters, or Venice of the East,' said Andrew.

Not a lot seemed to be happening, then Babaji said, 'We're just waiting for our two converted rice barges to be prepared for our journey down the canal and out across Lake Vembanad.'

Tabitha was standing next to Gloria, who was flapping her ears.

'A friend of mine once came on holiday here,' she said to Gloria.

'Oh,' said Gloria, still flapping her big ears.

'Yes, she was with her boyfriend. One evening they were

having dinner. He excused himself. He was gone for some time. She was just wondering where he had got to when he came back and popped the question.'

'What did she say?'

'Yes, of course. Then he gave her a ring woven from grass.'

'Is that what had taken him so long?'

'Yes, all that weaving takes time.'

'How romantic.'

'Yes, just imagine it – mattress on the foredeck, cotton sheets, goose-down pillows, voile curtains lifting in the breeze. What could be more romantic? That said, it is rather hot here, humid too, and there might be mosquitoes. So, now I come to think about it, I'd probably rather have a gold ring with a seal on it.'

Gloria looked down at the opal ring on the third toe of her left forefoot. 'Sounds more like a signet ring,' she said.

'That's what an engagement ring would have been originally, conferring the right to access one's husband's fortune on equal terms,' said Tabitha.

'How do you know that?'

'I heard it on the radio, on *Woman's Hour*, I think.'

'Sounds to me like a pre-nup of sorts. Would you have one of those?'

'Most certainly.'

'Why?'

'To protect my jewels, of course.'

'We can go aboard now,' said Andrew gruffly. Tabitha hoped she wasn't the reason for his bad mood and, desperately, that she was going to be on the same boat as him. Out of the corner of her eye she saw Babaji taking Kathleen, the hoolocks, the bison and the buffalo aboard one of the boats. Could be a good sign, she thought.

'Come this way,' said Andrew. Rhonda, Geraldine, Gloria and Tabitha followed him onto the other boat. He showed them to their cabins. In Tabitha's cabin, the one she was sharing with

Rhonda, there were two twin beds underneath a single mosquito net. Knowing that she was going to give Rhonda the mosquito net because Rhonda was an elderly rhino, Tabitha put her small green bag on one of the beds and went into the bathroom to freshen up.

When Tabitha emerged, Rhonda, Gloria and Geraldine were sitting on the foredeck in wicker chairs eating banana fritters from a silver platter. There was one left.

'Here,' said Gloria. But before Tabitha could get it, Rhonda ate it.

That's the last time I do something considerate for an elderly rhino, thought Tabitha.

The sides of the canal were made from stone and there were steps down to the water at regular intervals. Dhobi wallahs slapped wet fabric on to the stone. Slap, slap, slap, they went. The rice barges came to a bend in the canal. To the right there were palm trees silhouetted against a tangerine sky. To the left there were green paddy fields. Just after the bend, the two rice barges moored up end to end.

'You'll have to be patient,' said Andrew. 'It'll take some time for the cooks to prepare our evening meal.'

Tabitha went ashore and took some photos.

The hoolocks joined Andrew, Rhonda, Gloria, Geraldine and Tabitha aboard their rice barge. They meditated. Then they played cards. As it happened, Tabitha won every hand. Then, as the light faded, they ate by candlelight with citronella-scented mosquito coils burning at their feet.

'What is love?' said Henry out of the blue.

'I'm on the path but I don't know where I'm going,' said Andrew.

'I thought you were meant to be our guide,' said Henry.

A nervous titter ran round the group, but Andrew didn't smile.

'I feel as if I'm in two places at once,' he said.

'Heartbreaker,' said Rhonda.

Tabitha wondered then if her supposition about Rhonda had been right all along. If she was in love with Andrew, it would account for the fact that Rhonda wasn't speaking to her.

After dinner Tabitha was tidying up the aft deck, putting away the chairs, when Andrew approached her in the shadows. 'What do you think love is?' he asked.

'Let it rather be a moving sea between the shores of your souls,' she said.

'Kahlil Gibran,' said Andrew. 'It's easy to forget about him but he gets it spot on every time.'

'I agree.'

He helped Tabitha put away some chairs, then wandered off, saying 'Goodnight' over his shoulder.

While Rhonda was in the bathroom, Tabitha separated the two beds, giving Rhonda the mosquito net. She applied copious amounts of mosquito repellent to herself and waited for Rhonda to finish in the bathroom. Then, having completed her ablutions, she got into bed and tried to sleep. As on so many of the previous nights in India, sleep was hard to come by.

CHAPTER 11

The next day, Tabitha looked out of the porthole, bleary-eyed. A moorhen came out of the sedge and crossed the black water, leaving the shape of a 'V' in its wake. She did her teeth, especially her canines.

After breakfast they said goodbye to the canal and began their passage across Lake Vembanad. The sky was overcast, grey like the water, and there was a haze that made it difficult to see where the lake ended and the sky began. On the foredeck, Tabitha looked through her viewfinder. If her photographs were to be of interest to anyone other than herself, she would have to get closer to her subjects, she thought. Making her way up to the prow of the boat, she lay down and took photos of the big fat rice barges and the dugouts punted by stick-thin tall men.

Gloria and Babaji were sitting on the foredeck in wicker chairs. The elephant was flapping her big ears and waving her trunk.

'The barges are like whales,' said Tabitha. 'The dugouts are like minnows. If they don't watch out, they'll be swallowed alive.' Gloria and Babaji kept quiet. 'I wonder if the contribution to the economy made by the tourists outweighs the damage they do to the environment,' continued Tabitha.

'I wonder,' said Babaji and Gloria in unison.

'You mentioned that your father had two wives,' said Tabitha to Babaji.

Babaji avoided Tabitha's gaze. 'Yes,' he said in that ever so slightly quizzical way that suggested to Tabitha that he would rather have been the one doing the questioning. She was afraid that she had rattled what she feared to be his misogynist cage just a little too much. Time to back off, she thought. If she was to learn about his family's living arrangements, she was going to have to tread more carefully – adopt a subtler approach, in other words.

Late morning, they docked at a private jetty belonging to the Coconut Lagoon Hotel. Once they'd checked in, the porter showed Rhonda and Tabitha to their room, which was a thatched hut with a veranda. Tabitha went into the bathroom.

'The bathroom doesn't have a roof – just a palm tree at its centre,' she said.

Needless to say, Rhonda didn't reply, but just rubbed her horn with her forefoot.

In the bedroom, Tabitha changed into her bikini. She didn't want anybody spying on her in that roofless bathroom. Grabbing a towel, she headed for the pool. On the way, she came across lots of little bridges. In her opinion, there weren't enough of them in relation to the endless number of miniature canals.

She swam, and then sunbathed on a lounger next to Tracey.

'In case you didn't know, there's a formal dress code for lunch,' said Tracey.

'You should be careful,' said Eric. 'This sun is awfully strong.'

Fed up with the bisons' helpful suggestions, Tabitha moved to another sun lounger, which happened to be in the shade.

When she got back to the room, Rhonda had already gone to lunch, and Tabitha enjoyed a moment of solitude. Then, from her small green bag, she extracted a dress with its 'Cut Loose' label on the inside. She was just putting it on when there was a knock at the door. Who can that be? she wondered, but before she could get to the door, the door was flung open. A flurry of people came into the room. At the entrance, Rhonda was sitting in a wheelchair being pushed by Geraldine.

'One, two, three,' said Geraldine as she pushed Rhonda's considerable grey hulk over the threshold. Rhonda was ashen-faced, paler than any rhino Tabitha had ever seen. Also, she had a damp hairline and beads of sweat running down her neck dampening her salwar kameez. Geraldine pushed Rhonda towards the bed. Hotel staff gathered round.

'One, two, three,' said Geraldine, as she and the hotel staff heaved Rhonda out of the wheelchair and on to the bed.

Rhonda closed her eyes. Tabitha was afraid Rhonda was losing consciousness or – worst-case scenario – dying. Whatever, she thought, Rhonda needs privacy.

Tabitha went outside. Andrew was on the veranda, pacing up and down with his hands clasped behind his back.

'Is there anything I can do?' said Tabitha.

'Not really,' he said. 'You just go and have your lunch.'

Tabitha made straight for the buffet and piled her plate high with Indian goodies. The elephant, the pelican, the hoolocks, the bison and the buffalo were all sitting round a rectangular wooden table.

'You look nice,' said Tracey.

'What happened to Rhonda?' said Tabitha.

'You see that pit over there?' said Tracey. At the centre of the restaurant there was a decorative pit. 'Well, she fell into that.'

'It was awful,' said Gloria.

'She wasn't looking where she was going,' said Tracey. 'Too busy looking straight ahead at the buffet, I imagine.'

'Easy mistake to make,' said Kathleen, flapping her wings. 'I nearly did it myself.'

'Apparently, her CNS is normal,' said Tracey.

What's a CNS, thought Tabitha? Then she clicked – central nervous system.

66

'They're getting a MIMS list.'

'What's a MIMS list?' said Tabitha.

'An internationally recognised list of drugs,' said Tracey.

'I didn't know Rhonda was on drugs,' said Tabitha.

'Nor did we,' said Tracey.

'How did you manage to get her out of the pit?' said Tabitha.

'At first,' said Tracey, 'Geraldine and Clodagh, who used to be a nurse in A&E, tried to calm her. Then Henry had a go, but she wasn't having any of it, so in the end they had to sedate her.'

After lunch Tabitha went for a walk in the hotel grounds and came across a hammock. She tried settling herself in with a book, but she couldn't seem to concentrate. On the offchance that she might be able to get into her room, she headed back. On the way, she bumped into Gloria.

'We're going to meditate at five thirty in our room. If you'd like to join us, you'd be most welcome,' she said, swishing her tail from side to side.

'Thank you,' said Tabitha. 'That would be great.'

When she got back to her room, Andrew was still pacing up and down outside with his hands clasped behind his back.

'Please can I go in?' she said.

'If you're quiet as a church mouse,' he said.

Difficult for a tigress, she thought.

Changing into her bikini, she grabbed a towel, headed for the pool and swam. Then she went over to Gloria and Geraldine's room.

'You're punctual,' said Gloria.

The Andrew effect again, thought Tabitha. Even without looking at him, she blushed. He was already there, of course, sitting upright on a bamboo bench together with the hoolocks, Henry and Leticia. Geraldine and Gloria, too, were sitting upright on bamboo chairs. They all meditated for half an hour. When I say 'meditated', Tabitha's mind always seemed to gravitate in one direction – that of Andrew.

Afterwards there was no mention of Rhonda, which Tabitha found strange. Must be that stiff upper lip of Andrew's affecting them all, she thought.

'One of the girls from the hotel is going to show me how to put on a sari,' said Gloria. 'Would you like to come?'

'Yes please,' said Tabitha, recalling Gloria's acquisition of a sari for her daughter. Somebody's got to show her how to put it on, she thought. In fact, it's an elaborate process requiring the careful arrangement of what seems like at least one bolt of fabric round and round the body.

After learning how to put on a sari with Parvati, the animals, all bar Rhonda, went to a recital of Indian music in the grounds of the hotel. Tabitha didn't have a clue what the music was – maybe it was a raga from some south Indian province – but every time the sitar played, a family of ducks quacked – quack, quack, quack.

At dinner, Tabitha sat next to Andrew, opposite Geraldine.

'Describe your perfect home,' said Andrew.

'It would be a new build,' said Tabitha.

Andrew raised an eyebrow. 'Go on,' he said.

'It would be designed to nurture marital bliss,' she said.

'It's nine o'clock,' said Geraldine. 'You had better go and check on Rhonda.'

I'm not her skivvy, thought Tabitha.

'In what way?' said Andrew, ignoring Geraldine.

Tabitha was so cross with Geraldine that she couldn't think straight. Swishing her tail from side to side and baring her teeth, especially her canines, she said, 'In what way what?'

'Would a new build nurture marital bliss?' said Andrew.

'It would have separate bedrooms,' she said.

Andrew frowned.

'Absence makes the heart grow fonder,' she continued flirtatiously. 'Talking of which, I must go and attend to Rhonda.'

CHAPTER 12

At three o'clock in the morning the old-fashioned telephone on the far side of the rhino's bed rang. Tabitha leapt out of bed. She expected it to be Georgia, at home with the cat, returning her phone call of the previous afternoon. In the pitch black, she fumbled for the receiver and sat down cross-legged on the floor beside Rhonda's bed.

'Tabitha, Georgia here. Congratulations – you've got four healthy kittens – three boys and a girl.'

'Is Twinkle OK?'

'She's doing just fine.'

'When were they born?'

'First thing this morning.'

'Were you there?'

'No, she had them downstairs in the log basket.'

'What do they look like?'

'Tiny – the size of matchboxes – and completely hairless.'

'Thank you so much for birthing them and for looking after them – and their mother, of course. Are you all right?'

'Good, thank you.'

'Take care of yourself – and the cats, of course.'

'Will do.'

Tabitha put down the receiver with a heavy heart. She'd missed the high point of Twinkle's reproductive life. How could she have done? That said, she was truly grateful to have four healthy kittens and a healthy cat. How lucky was that? Just the thought of shared motherhood sent her head spinning. The excitement of it all! She could hardly contain herself.

At around nine o'clock Rhonda surfaced.

'Careful getting out of bed,' said Tabitha. 'If there's anything I can do, just let me know.'

Rhonda didn't reply. She went into the bathroom and from the noise – Niagara Falls, eat your heart out – Tabitha imagined a rhino peeing.

'You're a bit pale, but other than that you seem just fine,' said Tabitha, when Rhonda exited the bathroom. No response; she took it Rhonda was OK.

Tabitha skipped down the highways and byways of the Coconut Lagoon. Nothing, but nothing, could have dampened her spirits – not an inappropriate ratio of bridges to canals, nor an incommunicado rhino. She got into the dining room. She wasn't the first.

'I've got an announcement to make,' she said to the assembled animals in their party. 'I've had kittens. Oops, Freudian slip. What I meant to say was, my pet cat Twinkle's had kittens – three boys and a girl.'

There were one or two polite nods and smiles. To have said that Tabitha was disappointed by their indifference would have been far too understated; she was devastated.

After breakfast, their group was assembling on the bridge outside reception, getting ready for the off, when, waving a telephone bill, Rhonda approached.

'This is your share,' she said, pointing to by far the larger of two amounts.

That's funny, thought Tabitha. I only made one telephone call yesterday and Georgia was out. It can't be right. Then she saw that the larger of the two phone calls was in fact a call to Wales and must have been Rhonda's. Tabitha was just about to explain this to Rhonda when Rhonda, bless her big cotton socks, fell into conversation with Tracey.

'I spoke to my sister yesterday in Aberystwyth. It cost no more than an itemised phone call at home,' said Rhonda.

No point trying to explain to a rhino, thought Tabitha. I may as well just pay the bill and be done with it.

Tabitha went in search of Gloria and found her browsing in the gift shop. At first, they talked about the prices, then, when Tabitha could contain herself no longer, she started to talk about Rhonda.

'She hasn't spoken to me for virtually the whole tour. When she does speak, it's usually to herself, and she's just got herself in a terrible muddle over the phone bill,' said Tabitha.

'Have you told Geraldine?' said Gloria.

'No, this is the first time I've spoken to anybody about it.'

'You poor darling girl, keeping it all bottled up. You simply must speak to Geraldine about it.'

'Why?'

'Rhonda's on medication for psychosis. When she first arrived in India, she felt disoriented, so she doubled then quadrupled her dose without consulting a doctor. Anything untoward about her behaviour, you simply must tell Geraldine. She thinks it would be best to have Rhonda repatriated, but for some strange reason Andrew doesn't seem to think it would be a good idea.'

To be honest, the idea of having Rhonda repatriated filled Tabitha with delight, for without the rhino she imagined Andrew coming to her room.

'Something to do with maintaining integrity at the group level while expressing individuality at the rational level,' continued Gloria.

'What's that supposed to mean?'

'I'm not entirely sure,' said Gloria with a bemused smile.

Gloria was getting serious about her purchases, so Tabitha wandered out of the gift shop and sat down on the bench at reception. Eric came and sat next to her and she noticed Tracey staring daggers at them. Good grief, she thought, these animals. Being at home with the cats would be far easier.

'I think Rhonda is displaying the early signs of dementia,' he said.

'Have you told Geraldine?' said Tabitha.

'No.'

'Whyever not?'

'She's a doctor. I'm just a humble social worker.'

'Are you suggesting that she wouldn't listen to you because you're a social worker?'

'Yes.'

'Well, she's certainly formed a clique caring for Rhonda.'

'What do you mean by that?'

'Haven't you noticed? Geraldine, Tracey and Clodagh, healthcare professionals of one sort or another, all in it together.'

'I didn't realise Clodagh was a healthcare professional.'

'She used to be a nurse in A&E.'

A motor launch with a canvas awning arrived at the side of the reception bridge, and one by one the hotel staff helped the animals aboard.

Callum sat down next to Tabitha. 'I hear you've had kittens,' he said.

At last, a buffalo who appreciates the birth of the Twinklets, thought Tabitha, regaling Callum with the story of how Twinkle came to give birth, down to the last detail. He listened attentively. Insofar as she could tell though, Andrew wasn't listening. In spite of her performance – for that is what it was – he wasn't paying her the slightest bit of attention.

This made Tabitha feel very depressed. If Andrew wasn't interested in the Twinklets then, by implication, he wasn't interested in her. Maybe he thought she was past it – that there wouldn't be any cubs for her. But she was only just forty-one; there was plenty of time for her offspring, if only he would get a move on. She stared at the sides of the canal and bit back the tears, trying to console herself with thoughts of the joint parenting she would be doing with Twinkle.

There would be no more slapping of wet fabric here. The sides of this canal were made from clay and it looked like a dredger might have been through recently – either that or a giant cheese cutter.

The motor launch moored up alongside a wooden jetty, which led to a tarmac road. Parked to one side was their bus. Just the sight of it, all alone, made Tabitha want to cry some more. She made her way to her seat, one row from the back on the left-hand side. She looked out of the window and let the tears roll.

On their way to the Western Ghats, they passed through plantation country.

'I'm about to administer another of my sleeping pills,' said Andrew. 'This time it's about the Raj.'

Tabitha fell asleep. When she woke up, they were just arriving at the next hotel. Talk about perfect timing.

'If you follow the track up the hill,' said Andrew, 'you'll come to a gate on the left-hand side. Go through the gate and there's a bridge. Cross the bridge and you'll come to the reception area of the Shalimar Spice Garden Hotel.'

Tabitha walked to the front of the bus to where Andrew and Babaji were standing.

'Looks like you're abandoning us animals,' she said.

'Would we?' said Babaji.

'Would we ever?' said Andrew. 'It's just that we can't leave the coach here. We have to go further down the hill to the car park. We'll see you shortly in reception.'

The animals walked along the track. A five-bar gate, elm saplings and willow herb sprouting from the hedgerow made the tigress think of England. If it hadn't been for the peppercorns drying in the field on black plastic sacks, they could have been there. Gloria flapped her big ears, waved her trunk and pointed to her left.

'That must be the hotel,' she said.

'Where?' said Tabitha.

'Look over there – the Chinese gate.'

And just when I was beginning to feel at home in India, she thought. On the other side of the gate, there was a slatted bridge suspended by ropes over a ravine. The animals crossed gingerly, holding on to the rope 'balustrade'. The reception area was a platform, supported by wooden struts, which projected out into the ravine. As if from nowhere, Andrew, Babaji and their luggage met them. At the reception desk, they checked in.

'Lunch is at one, so if you'd like to go to your rooms and come straight back to the dining room we can eat.'

'Yes, sir,' said Tabitha under her breath.

'What was that?' said Babaji. Not so under her breath as she'd hoped.

'Nothing,' she said. She picked up her small green bag. The porter picked up the rhino's two enormous suitcases. They followed the porter. He wended his way along a winding path that led up the hill through woodland until they got to a row of wooden chalets. Theirs was the last one. Tabitha tipped him. Rhonda and Tabitha unpacked, then they walked together in silence to the outside dining area.

At lunch they were sitting on wooden benches that were slightly too far away from the wooden table for comfort. Because of their concrete legs, they couldn't be moved. They reminded Tabitha of the group and its members, stuck too far away from each other for comfort.

Back in the room, Tabitha got out the *South India Handbook*, a present given to her by her mother for Christmas. With a view to separating herself from the group and travelling alone, she looked at the chapters on Kerala and Tamil Nadu. She imagined herself saying to Andrew that she was thinking of leaving, but for some reason she couldn't quite do it. She decided to go for a walk. The fresh air would do her good, she thought, and might even help her make up her mind. To stay or to go, that was the question.

Tabitha prowled the perimeter fence and found a hole. She squeezed through the hole and looked about her. She was on a well-worn dirt path bordered by hibiscus and laurel hedging. She followed the path. It led her past small fields and mud huts into a village, where children were playing on either side of a newly tarmacked road. Villagers stood in darkened doorways. She waved at them; they waved back.

As she left the village there was a sharp bend in the road, and a shrine. She lit a candle, and a man on a scooter overtook her. Traversing the hill opposite, there was a track. It left the road, and she followed it. The scooter that had overtaken her was parked where the track narrowed to a grass path. Up ahead she could see the man who had been riding the scooter. He was standing in a glade of silver birches. She couldn't see the finer detail but something about his stance, a certain projection from the pelvic region, the position and rhythmic movement of his hand, the gormless expression on his face, then a toothless grin, made her think he was masturbating.

She hesitated. This man might attack her. He might even rape her. Then again, she thought, by the time I pass by, he will have ejaculated. Even so, she needed to be careful. On the other hand, why should she let this man's desire to get his rocks off in the presence of a Western tigress interfere with her plans? She walked on by and passed the man without incident. Thank goodness for that, she thought. The grass path narrowed even more and became a steep path edged with brambles. She rounded a corner. A group of young girls were chattering away in Malayalam.

'Hi there,' said Tabitha in English. The girls giggled. One of them got her a small red plastic chair to sit on. Another got her a cup of sweet Indian tea. Tabitha worried the water may not have been boiled, then she thought, What the hell. The gesture was kind and the tea would be delicious.

One of the girls spoke English. 'The youngest amongst us is getting married in the morning,' she said.

'Congratulations,' said Tabitha.

'Would you like to come to the wedding?' said the youngest girl in Malayalam. The girl who spoke English translated.

'I'd love to,' said Tabitha. 'Where shall we meet?'

'Here.'

'Until tomorrow, then.'

Tabitha retraced her steps back to the hotel without getting lost, and was very proud of herself for doing so. When she got back, there was a folded piece of paper on her pillow. She unfolded it. 'Gloria the elephant and Geraldine the glang request the pleasure of your company at their chalet at six o'clock,' it said.

Tabitha looked at her watch. It was just after five. There was time for a swim. Climbing the hill to the pool – more like a plunge pool – she swam one hundred lengths and got out. Wrapping herself in a towel as if it were a strapless dress, she considered herself suitably attired for drinks, and made her way to Gloria and Geraldine's chalet for ten past six. The door was ajar.

'Anybody in?' she said.

'We're in here,' said Gloria. 'Come on in and take a pew.'

Tabitha took it Gloria meant for her to sit on the end of the bed. Gloria, sitting at a dressing room table, was wearing a grey silk shirt and a paisley pleated skirt. Looking in the mirror, she applied plum-coloured lipstick, placed a tissue between her lips and smacked them together. She reminds me of my mother, thought Tabitha.

'Won't be a moment,' called Geraldine from behind the closed bathroom door. When she emerged, she was wearing a black plunge bra and black pants, and sporting a turban made from a towel.

No wonder she's been receiving telephone calls from her lover, thought Tabitha.

'Now, young lady,' said Geraldine when she emerged, 'to be perfectly honest, we're worried about you. You're obviously finding it difficult to share with a rhino, so we've come up with a plan. We thought it might be a good idea if you spent a couple of nights in a room of your own, so what do you think?'

Tabitha didn't like the inference that it was somehow her fault that she was finding it difficult to share with a rhino. She did, however, like the idea of having a room to herself. 'Sounds like a plan,' she said. 'But how are we going to convince Rhonda it's a good idea?'

'You'll think of something and we'll sort it with Andrew,' said Gloria.

'Can I go now?'

'Not before we've opened a bottle of champagne to celebrate, and you've told us how you spent your afternoon.'

Tabitha recounted the story of how she had spent her afternoon. Gloria and Geraldine ooohed and ahhed in all the right places. Then Tabitha asked them how they spent their afternoons.

'I watched telly,' said Gloria.

'What did you watch?' said Tabitha.

'Indian soaps.'

Back in their room, Rhonda was having a lie down.

'I'm not feeling very well,' said Tabitha.

Rhonda didn't say anything, but just rubbed her horn with her forefoot. No surprises there.

'I was thinking of getting a room on my own until I recover.'

Rhonda sat up and beamed like Tabitha had never seen a rhino beam.

At dinner, the head waiter approached with a message. 'Andrew's waiting for you in reception,' he said.

Tabitha's heart skipped a beat. She wanted to be fashionably late, so she fiddled with her cutlery. She was just pushing her chair back, about to get up, when she caught sight of Andrew in the doorway. His brow was wrinkled and he looked a bit uptight, as if he couldn't bear waiting any longer.

'I'll be right there,' she said.

Andrew turned his back. Tabitha took the opportunity of saluting Gloria and Geraldine, just to let them know that everything was going according to plan. Tabitha followed Andrew into the reception area. Babaji was there.

'Take a seat,' said Andrew.

'How's it going?' said Babaji.

'Good, except for you know who,' said Tabitha, swishing her tail.

'I understand from the glang that you would like a room of your own,' said Andrew, a little too formally for Tabitha's liking. 'Is that right?'

'Yes.'

'Your wish is my command,' he replied.

Easy as that? Tabitha couldn't believe her luck.

'You'll have to pay the single supplement, of course.'

'But of course,' she said, when what she actually thought was this: That's not fair – it's not my fault I got to share with a psychotic rhino who's quadrupled the dose of her medication without consulting a doctor, and who fell into the decorative pit at the centre of a restaurant. You're the tour guide; you've got to take some responsibility for this.

'Would you like to see your room?' said Andrew.

'Yes please,' was all she said.

Andrew, hands clasped behind his back, left reception. Babaji and Tabitha followed. They wended their way through woodland, past the path that led to Rhonda's chalet, onwards until they got to a clearing. In the middle there was a big rectangular wooden box the size of a room. It was covered in carvings of gods, goddesses, exotic animals and wild beasts. In the middle of one of the long sides there was a set of steps, which Andrew climbed, and a door with a padlock. Andrew unlocked it. They went in. It was so beautiful Tabitha could hardly believe it. Voile curtains hung on brass poles at the shuttered windows. Sheepskin rugs softened the terracotta-tiled floor. The bed was simply made up with white linen sheets and a red blanket.

'The bridal suite, all to yourself,' said Andrew.

'Well, you're both welcome to join me whenever you like,' said Tabitha. Talk about Freudian slip. She blushed big time, red right to the roots of her black and orange striped fur.

'One condition,' said Andrew. 'You don't tell anyone.'

'Why not?'

'They'll all be wanting one.'

They all laughed.

'Let's go to the bar. I'll buy you a drink,' said Andrew.

The bar was heaving.

'What would you like?' said Andrew.

'A Tiger beer,' said Tabitha.

Andrew and Babaji hung around for a while, then they disappeared. They must have unfinished business to attend to, thought Tabitha, and tried not to take their departure too personally. She hated being left in a bar on her own. Luckily, it wasn't long before Geraldine rescued her.

'Tell them about your afternoon,' she said – 'them' as in the pelican, the hoolocks, the bison and the buffalo.

'Are you actually going to go to the wedding?' said Tracey.

'Yes,' said Tabitha.

'You can't do that – not on your own,' said Tracey.

I bloody well can and I bloody well am, thought Tabitha.

'You'll have to tell Andrew,' continued Tracey.

As luck would have it, Andrew and Babaji were just passing. Tabitha was afraid that their reactions would be as violent as Tracey's, and the hairs on the back of her neck stood up.

'I'll organise for a guide to go with you from the hotel,' said Andrew.

Thank goodness for that, thought Tabitha – not that she particularly wanted a guide to go with her, but at least she could go. She said goodnight to the group.

'Don't do anything I wouldn't do,' said Callum.

Tabitha was heading in the direction of the bridal suite. In keeping with her promise to Andrew, she was alone. Then Tracey fell into step with her. Try as she might, Tabitha couldn't seem to shake her off. They got to the bridal suite.

'Is this where you're staying?' said Tracey.

'Yes,' said Tabitha.

'Can I have a look?'

Tabitha couldn't very well say no, not to a violent female bison, but she couldn't believe that she'd just broken her first ever promise to Andrew. How bad was that? Tracey and Tabitha looked round the bridal suite. Tracey oohed, and not just the once.

CHAPTER 13

Tabitha looked at her watch. It was eight o'clock in the morning. Light slipped through the shutters and into the bridal suite. What with her ablutions, meditation, breakfast, etcetera, meeting the bride at nine was going to be tight.

Geraldine was just leaving the dining room as Tabitha was entering it. Their paths crossed.

'Young lady, I'm assuming you're going to be accompanied this morning,' said Geraldine.

To be honest, Tabitha had hoped that interest in her antics would have died down by now, that she'd be free to go on her own.

Rhonda was breakfasting alone.

'Do you mind if I join you?' said Tabitha. Rhonda didn't reply – no surprises there. Tabitha took her silence as a 'no, I don't mind' and sat down. Gloria appeared and sat down next to the rhino. Andrew and Babaji joined them. Andrew sat down next to Tabitha and Babaji sat down next to Gloria. Rhonda withdrew. Andrew put his hand on Tabitha's thigh. Here's hoping he doesn't move it on up, she thought, because she wasn't wearing any knickers.

'What is it with you and authority?' he said, squeezing her thigh.

'I'm working on it,' she said.

'How?' She was just about to give Andrew a long explanation of how she was working on her authority issues when he launched into an explanation of his own.

'There simply is more energy in the tropics,' he said, 'energy that's dispersed at regular festivals.'

Tabitha wanted to tell him that she may have been just forty-one but that she was a tigress who'd read Anthropology at university and that she was very well travelled. She'd even been to Antarctica.

'Added to which,' he went on, 'the media encourages the average Indian man to see Western women as loose, especially with their VPLs.'

For a moment, Tabitha couldn't think what Andrew was on about, then she clicked – visible panty lines. She hadn't heard that initialism for a while. I'm not a woman and I haven't got a VPL, she wanted to say.

'So someone from the hotel really should go with you this morning. If you go to reception, the manager will arrange it.'

'I take it that's a command,' said Tabitha.

Andrew didn't say a thing – just looked into her eyes and beamed.

What it is to have one's sense of humour appreciated, she thought. 'I'll go to reception,' she said.

Andrew's hand slipped discreetly off her thigh. She looked at her watch. It was five to nine.

'I'm going to a wedding this morning. Andrew said that you might be able to provide me with an escort?' said Tabitha to the receptionist of the hotel.

'Anything you say, memsahib, but in India weddings don't take place on a Friday,' said the receptionist.

For a moment Tabitha doubted herself, then she repeated her request. A young local man appeared from behind the desk. Looking him up and down, she tried to get the measure of him.

'Tabitha,' she said, holding out her paw.

'Agi,' he said, shaking her paw.

'Let's go.'

'Weddings in India never take place on a Friday.'

Again, Tabitha's confidence was shaken. Also, she couldn't seem to remember where she was supposed to be meeting the bride. All of a sudden an elderly man appeared.

'We were wondering where you'd got to. James, the bride's father.'

Could James really be his name? Tabitha wondered. He looks pretty local to me, she thought.

'Delighted to meet you,' she said. 'I'm sorry we're late. I wasn't entirely sure I'd got the right day. Agi here said that Indian weddings never take place on a Friday.'

'This is a Pentecostal wedding. They always take place on a Friday.'

Tabitha was relieved – at least there was a wedding to go to – and disappointed – it wasn't a Hindi wedding. She tried to hide her disappointment, because she didn't want to cause offence.

'Follow me,' said James.

Agi and Tabitha walked alongside James. She soon began to recognise the landmarks. Round the next corner, and they were where the bride had told her to meet them. She could hardly believe her eyes. Coming down the hill on the steep grass path, as if it were a tarmac road, were two vehicles. The first was a white Ambassador and the second was a beige jeep. The vehicles stopped and the doors opened. Inside the Ambassador was the bride. She could only have been about fifteen. She was wearing a red silk sari embroidered with gold. Surrounding her was a group of women wearing saris in a range of colours from blue and green to purple, pink and violet. Tabitha's paw went immediately to the camera hung round her neck. She didn't want to intrude without asking, so she said, 'May I?'

Everyone nodded in the affirmative – no surprises there. What it was to have one's photo taken by a tigress – the kudos of it all. Through the lens of her camera, again and again Tabitha met their serious faces.

Then James said, 'If you'd like to step up on to the tailgate…'

They set off, rumbling over rough ground. The roll bar was hidden under the tarpaulin roof of the jeep. Finding it, Tabitha clung on for dear life and looked around.

Agi and James were jumping on and off the jeep as they stopped and started. Tabitha threw back her head. What it was to be free, free of the luxury hotels they had been staying in, free, free to enjoy the real India beyond their well-watered grounds.

They came to a small track, then a road through a village. Tabitha was feeling disoriented and hadn't a clue where she was. The vehicles came to a standstill. Everyone was disgorged, including the bride. There was work to be done, namely smoothing her sari, positioning and repositioning her diamante and gold tiara as well as her short white lace veil, and tweaking her bouquet of red and white carnations and feathery green ferns.

'Ready to go,' said James.

They proceeded round the side of the church, the happy couple at the front and Tabitha and James at the back. Underfoot was a narrow, hard, worn dirt path. To either side were hibiscus and laurel hedges. The church was a dilapidated, ramshackle, one-storey affair painted turquoise, but the paint was peeling. James ushered Tabitha into a small room.

'My bedroom,' he said proudly. Tabitha didn't know what to say, so she looked at the floor, blushed and hoped James didn't have a wife to speak of, as she wouldn't want to upset her.

Inside the church was a white rectangular room with a low ceiling.

'Sit down here,' said James.

Tabitha sat on the floor and saw that there were men on one

side of the room and women on the other, and that she'd been deemed an honorary man. She slid on her bottom across to the women's side, where she was offered a chair. Declining, she slid, again on her bottom to the back of the room and leaned against the wall. The service was being conducted in Malayalam so she didn't understand a word. What she did do was cover her head with the hood of her photographer's gilet at the same time as the women covered their heads with their saris. But then, all of a sudden, there was no more taking a low profile for her; she was hauled out of the congregation and told to stand next to the bride and groom.

'Say cheese,' said the official photographer. As well as the photographer, there was an official video cameraman with lots of bright lights, making a film of proceedings.

For the reception, Tabitha was accompanied by James – but of course. Outside the church, there were lots of young children pressing posies into her paws. She felt like a queen. They followed the path back down to the road and turned left. Tabitha was just getting into her regal stride, surrounded by men, women and children, when, from behind, there was an almighty honk.

Bearing down on them like a thug was the bus. Tabitha couldn't believe it – just when she'd got away from all that. We must be in the vicinity of the spice garden, she thought. What an unwelcome coincidence. The bus looked enormous. Tabitha peered up at the windows and tried to see in, but the sunlight was reflecting on the glass so she couldn't see a thing. Just the thought of Andrew and all the others staring down at them made her feel sick. She kept on striding down the road just as fast as her legs would carry her. After what seemed like an age, the bus passed by and they were left in peace to enjoy their freedom.

They came to a track on the left which led into a field.

'It's going to be a church,' said James. He was referring to a half-built structure comprising three breeze-block walls, a concrete floor and a roof of sorts.

In spite of the open side, they went in through a door. A U-shaped banqueting table had been set up. At each setting, there was a white plastic cup filled with a pink fluorescent liquid, a paper plate covered in droplets of water and a black boiled sweet wrapped in cellophane. James showed Tabitha to her place. Unwrapping her sweet, she sucked on it and wiped her plate clean on her dress. She needn't have bothered cleaning her plate; two young waiters wearing white shirts and black trousers used their hands to dollop two great mounds, one of curry and the other of rice, onto it. She used a plastic knife and fork for her main course and a plastic spoon for her pudding – tinned fruit salad with lashings of bright yellow custard.

'What's your name?' said Tabitha to her neighbour.

'Sanjay,' he said.

'How do you know the bride and groom?'

Unfortunately, Sanjay didn't speak much English, so he couldn't answer her question.

Through the open side of the will-be-church, Tabitha took in the view: green fields, barbed wire, the odd oak tree. If it hadn't been for the pelican – the pelican? The tigress did a double take – We could be in England, she thought. What's the pelican doing here? she wondered. What's more, how did she inveigle her way in? How dare she, when I did the donkey work, she thought, getting to know the bride and all that? This was her territory.

Tabitha got up and went for a prowl. Coming across a queue to have her paws washed, she stood in line and, when she got to the head of the queue, had her paws scrubbed by a woman who only spoke Malayalam. Afterwards she dried them on a well-used beige towel that hung from a tree, and took photographs. One in particular was of a little girl wearing a pink dress and holding a melting ice-cream that was running down her deeply veined hands in rivulets.

Tabitha bumped into James.

'When are you thinking of going?' she said.

'In the next half hour,' said James, wagging his head from side to side. Tabitha didn't know whether to believe him, so she took matters into her own paws. She scrambled through a barbed wire fence, made her way along a track and came to the road. The bus was there. It looked to Tabitha as though it must have been waiting for the other animals while they enjoyed their trip to the spice garden. She hopped aboard.

After a while the bus driver said to her, 'What are you doing?'

'Waiting for the others,' she said.

'They're back at the hotel having lunch,' said the bus driver.

The penny dropped. They weren't anywhere near the spice garden. They were back at the hotel. In point of fact, they'd never been far from the hotel – certainly not in the vicinity of the spice garden. Talk about disoriented. Imagine if she'd tried to leave the group? She didn't imagine she would have got very far on her own.

At lunch Tabitha gave the group an account of how she'd spent her morning. The animals told her about the spice garden and how much she would have enjoyed it, given her profession as garden designer.

Andrew was talking to Gloria across the table. Tabitha envied her. She would have liked to be talking to Andrew. They were talking about *A Passage to India*. She wasn't as educated in that department as Gloria. All she could think about re *A Passage to India* was the hot and steamy sex in the film or could she, she wasn't even sure if she'd got that right.

Tabitha always kept a note in her diary of the day she was on in her cycle. Today was day ten. From here on in, she was at her most fertile.

That afternoon, they went into the jungle proper. Up above, howler monkeys were screeching. The hoolocks whoopoo-whooped.

'Neoteny,' said Tabitha.

'Neoto-what?' said Andrew. He was walking beside her. Close.

'Neoteny is the retention of juvenile characteristics in the adult form. It accounts for people's big brains, which go on growing in the early years after they're born – unlike the great apes with whom humans share ninety-nine per cent of their genetic material.'

'Hmmmm,' said Andrew.

On their return from the jungle they swung by a lake. In the car park there were wild boar rootling around for acorns. Outside the sanctuary there was also a spice shop. They stopped off and rootled around themselves. With its spotless white walls and shiny black tiled floor and glass cabinets, it looked more like a chemist's than a spice shop, but the aroma was of spice. Tabitha selected two variety packs: long cellophane strips divided into compartments. Both were for cooks in her family: her sister-in-law and her father. She also selected black peppercorns, vanilla pods, cinnamon sticks and mace for herself, as well as saffron in a tiny Petri dish for her friend Iona. She took her spices to the woman at the electronic till with its bright green digits. The bill was much more than she expected. Why Andrew hadn't just taken them to a local market beat her. But he did buy two of the same spices as her, and she took this as an auspicious sign with regard to their future domestic bliss.

Next door to the spice shop there was a boutique selling clothes, jewellery and household furnishings, which were more Tabitha's kind of thing. Also, now she'd been in India for more than a week, she could safely say she'd got her shopping eye, so she could distinguish tat from the real McCoy. She'd learned about how to bargain and she knew what she wanted. A moonstone necklace like Gloria's would do nicely, thank you. She spotted one, a large moonstone beneath three smaller ones, all set in the most delicate filigree.

The shopkeeper handed her an elegant oval mirror with a smooth wooden handle. 'Suits you,' he said.

Tabitha looked at herself. 'How much?' she said.

'For you, memsahib, thirty-five thousand rupees.'

That was fifty quid. Way over budget. The shopkeeper didn't look like the bargaining type. Unclasping the necklace with care, Tabitha handed it to the shopkeeper and left the shop.

Back at the hotel, Andrew and Babaji collared her for the single supplement. Without so much as a murmur, she coughed up. Then she bounded up the hill to the pool for a swim. Gloria was sitting on a sun lounger.

'Tea for two,' she said to a passing waiter.

'This heat,' said the tigress.

The tea arrived.

'That's better,' said Gloria, using her trunk to sip her tea and waving her ears to create a breeze.

'I can't imagine why Tracey and Eric got so upset about my going to that wedding,' said Tabitha. 'It's not as if I'm a schoolgirl.'

'No,' said Gloria.

'I'm a fully fledged forty-one-year-old tigress. That said, I hope I didn't threaten the integrity of the group by doing my own thing.'

'Whatever do you mean?'

'Well, don't you remember Andrew saying it was important not to threaten the integrity of the group?'

'Yes, I do, but that was in relation to Rhonda and us animals wanting her to be repatriated – nothing to do with you. You, my dear, can do anything you want. Don't worry about what Andrew thinks. Just remember, you're on holiday and you can do as you please.'

After dinner they retired to the front lobby of the hotel. With its white walls, terracotta-tiled floor and tall, thin, rectangular glass cases displaying jewellery, it was all very swish. In keeping with her surroundings, the maitre d' of the hotel was floating between the display cases in a black diaphanous outfit. Tabitha was perched on a bench at the side of the room between Gloria and Geraldine.

'I've a suggestion to make,' said Geraldine. 'For the remainder of the tour, wherever we can, us three should share a room.'

Gloria seconded the proposal.

There goes my tryst with Andrew, thought Tabitha.

'When we get back, I'm taking to the slopes with my lover,' said Geraldine. Tabitha imagined the glang on skis, whizzing down the mountain.

'I'm going skiing too, although not with my lover – with some friends.'

'What's happening with your career?' said Geraldine.

'Not much,' said Tabitha. 'Would you like to have a look at the bridal suite now?'

'Yes please,' said Gloria and Geraldine.

They trooped up the hill. In the bridal suite there was lots of oohing and aahing, especially when it came to the bathroom where Gloria and Geraldine got into the bath fully clothed. They pretended to scrub and wash themselves.

'You had better make sure the shutters are closed,' said Gloria. 'We don't want a tiger carrying you off now, do we?'

Now there's a thought, thought the tigress.

'No,' she said, more preoccupied with the possibility that Andrew might come to her, especially now she had a room of her own.

CHAPTER 14

Before Tabitha knew it, and much to her disappointment because Andrew hadn't come to her room during the night, it was morning and there was a loud knock at the door. She'd been expecting an alarm call.

'Who's there?' she said.

'The porter.'

'Couldn't you come back in half an hour?'

No time to meditate. In the pitch black, she tried to open the shutters. No luck – they were stuck. She gave them a shove. Open sesame – they gave; there was light and she packed.

Rhonda was breakfasting alone in the dining room. In front of her, there was a pile of knickers. The tigress assumed that the knickers were clean, having just been returned from the laundry.

'How are you?' she said on the off chance that Rhonda might be speaking to her.

'I didn't sleep,' said Rhonda.

Tabitha did a double take; Rhonda was actually speaking to her.

'I am sorry,' said Tabitha.

'I woke up at two thirty this morning with terrible pains in my ribs.'

'Perhaps you should see a doctor,' ventured Tabitha.

Tabitha sat in her normal seat, curled up, tail tucked in, and the bus climbed through woodland up on to a plateau of weather-beaten granite. At the far edge, through haze, she could see the plain stretching out below them.

'There's a shrine coming up by the side of the road,' said Andrew. 'Time for a chai stop.'

When they got out, Tabitha took a photo of a figure in an orange coat against a backdrop of green banana leaves and red soil.

'We're on our way to Madurai, so I'm going to administer another of my sleeping pills,' said Andrew. 'Your first taste of Tamil Nadu,' he continued. 'Where history, the passage of the ego, meets myth, the journey of the soul.' The mere mention of the word 'myth' made the anthropologist in Tabitha think of Lévi-Strauss, who argued that the structure of myth reflected the dualistic structure of the brain. It also made her think of Adam Phillips, who argued that our inability to face death gives rise to mythical stories purporting to human immortality. Tabitha would have liked to talk to Andrew about these things, but he was too busy, of course, putting everybody else to sleep.

The bus swept through iron gates and brick pillars into a curved drive. Descending, they arrived in the lobby of the Taj Garden Retreat, which smelled of must. The cushions of the cane chairs were upholstered in floral linen. They sat down and staff brought them ice-cold water.

Tabitha raised her tumbler. 'To the faded glory of the Raj,' she said.

'I bet that layer of haze floating above the city wasn't there in those days,' said Eric.

Tracey stared daggers at Tabitha again. What a killjoy,

thought Tabitha. Even though Tabitha wasn't sitting with Gloria and Geraldine, she could hear what they were saying.

'I'm worried sick about Rhonda,' said Geraldine.

'Me too,' said Gloria.

'She woke me at seven thirty this morning to say she couldn't breathe,' said Geraldine.

'Sounds to me as if she needs to be repatriated as soon as humanly possible,' said Gloria.

'I agree,' said Geraldine.

'Have you said anything to Andrew?' said Gloria.

'Not recently. At least now he's going to have her examined by a local doctor.'

'When?'

'This evening.'

'Then he's sure to change his mind.'

Here's hoping, thought Tabitha.

Porters appeared.

'The three of you who are sharing a room, if you'd like to follow me,' said one of them.

The narrow concrete paths that led through the hotel were painted red and edged with *Lonicera nitida*. They came to a terracotta-tiled stairwell and descended to the room at the bottom. The porter tried the key.

'It's the wrong one,' he said. 'I'll have to go back to reception. If you don't mind waiting, I won't be a minute.'

Gloria tapped the side of her trunk. 'Phone calls have been made,' she said. 'Rhonda will soon be going back to London.'

'Really,' said Tabitha.

'Yes, it's just that they've had difficulty getting through to the insurance company.'

In this day and age, Tabitha wondered.

'Won't be long now before she's on her way home.'

*

Let's hope so, thought Tabitha.

The bedroom was big, with one double bed and a single bed under the window. There was lots of oohing and aahing, then Geraldine said she'd take the single bed, leaving Tabitha to share the double bed with an elephant. I ask you. After unpacking, they partook of a little light lunch. Then they sunbathed and swam before – guess what? – visiting another temple.

At the entrance, known as a gopuram, there was an elephant, and as Henry approached it the elephant placed its trunk on top of Henry's head and gently stroked it. But all of a sudden the elephant gave an almighty sneeze. Tabitha had never seen so much mucus, and nor had Henry, or so it seemed from the fuss that he made, forearms flapping all over the place. Tabitha felt sorry for the elephant, whose watery grey eyes looked unhappy, as they do at the best of times. The elephant must have wondered what on earth all the commotion was about.

Inside the temple there were rows of lungi-clad young boys, sitting cross-legged on the floor and learning how to chant. There was also a set of giant granite steps leading down to a pool of brackish water strewn with litter and surrounded by pale blue railings. It was hot, and if it hadn't been for the litter, Tabitha would have felt like going for a dip.

Further into the interior of the temple, there was what looked like a dead tree. Hanging from the branches by threads, to which frayed pieces of fabric had been knotted, were little cribs. Andrew beckoned Tabitha over.

'It's a fertility shrine,' he said.

'Is it?' said Tabitha, blushing. Secretly she was thinking, If it isn't too late, I'd like to have cubs. She prayed for the as-yet-unborn cubs.

Andrew walked off.

Tabitha followed, and they entered an inner sanctum hewn from rock. The thought of all that rock above her, especially the weight, made her feel anxious. Incense smouldered. There was a cacophony of sound, marked as always by the rattle of the tambourine. Brown-bodied young men, whose torsos were covered in a fine layer of sweat, bore glowing oil lamps trailing black smoke. They joined a continuous stream of devotees – local Tamils, Tabitha imagined – who were making their way to the inner core of the temple, where black wooden figures stood in a series of shrines behind black railings. At the foot of each figure there were offerings of food and flowers – some fresh, others not so. There was a rotten stench and, as the temperature rose and the atmosphere darkened, it was as if they were in hell.

'Thou shalt have no other God,' rang in Tabitha's mind.

Outside the temple, Tabitha took a deep breath of fresh air. She was in a world of her own, contemplating her experience of the temple.

'How was it for you?' said Andrew, taking her aback.

'To be honest, I feel harrowed, and it reminds me of Nepal.'

'The same raw energy of the shamanistic societies of the north,' said Andrew, beaming. He had obviously relished the experience.

Tabitha collapsed on the back seat of the bus, exhausted. The bus angled its way through the bent streets of Madurai, up the hill to the reassuringly solid gates of the Taj Retreat. Time for a dip, a sunbathe and a little light supper, thought Tabitha.

'Rhonda's been examined,' said Geraldine in a low voice over supper.

'What news?' said Gloria.

'She's not being repatriated,' said Geraldine.

'Whyever not?' said Tabitha.

'Well, the local doctor obviously didn't think she was bad enough, and Andrew still doesn't want her to go,' said Geraldine.

'Ridiculous!' said Gloria.

Towards the end of supper, Andrew asked if anyone would like to go to the evening's arati.

'What's an arati?' said Tabitha.

'A procession headed by a cow and an elephant in which Siva, Minakshi's consort, is carried round the temple, ultimately to sleep at her side.'

'Who's Minakshi?'

'The fish-eyed goddess, the only goddess to preside over a southern Indian temple.'

Not another bloody temple, thought Tabitha at first. Then she thought, How refreshing, the power of the feminine. Maybe that will make me feel a little more relaxed.

CHAPTER 15

Next morning, at seven thirty, Tabitha woke up. Gloria was meditating and Geraldine had left the room. Everybody seems to be going about their business except me, thought Tabitha, and I'm too knackered even to get out of bed. Rolling over, she went back to sleep.

After breakfast at nine, she gathered her things and headed up a slope for the bus. Andrew was coming towards her.

'Namaste,' he said.

'Namaste,' she replied.

Then he took her in his arms. He said, 'I salute all the divine qualities in you, my proud empress.'

She could feel the rumble of her camera down her right forearm. The camera was threatening to hit the ground. In order to save it, she would have to grab it with her left paw. This made for an awkward embrace. Still, it was their first public embrace and, though it may have been awkward, it had to be savoured.

Thankfully, there was time on the bus to do so. Outside a shop on East Chattel Street, they came to a halt alongside a hawker selling peacock feathers. Tabitha wanted to buy one.

'You may be wondering why we've stopped here,' said Andrew. 'It's because there's a roof terrace from where we can get a bird's-eye view of the temple. And don't think I've forgotten your shopaholic tendencies. If there's anything you like the look of on your way up through the shop, then you can be safe in the knowledge that we'll be coming back here after we've visited the temple.'

The animals descended from the bus and climbed the stairs up through the shop. At the top, seen from the roof terrace, there were aerials galore.

'If you look carefully, you'll see that the four gopurams that mark the entrances to the temple are made from colourful stucco decorated with images of gods, goddesses and animals,' said Andrew. 'I'd also like you to look at the vimanas – five massive sanctuaries where the deities are housed.'

They looked, and then climbed back down to street level.

'We'll be entering the temple through the Ashta Sakthi Mandapam, or porch of the eight goddesses,' said Andrew. 'To the left of the porch, you'll see there's a small canvas shack where you can leave your shoes.'

The shoe shelves were the most chaotic Tabitha had seen on this trip thus far. She was loath to take off her pointed black suede slip-ons, given to her by her mother, a Christmas present from Caroline Charles in Beauchamp Place. But as everyone else was doing so, she did the same.

Andrew introduced the animals to a local guide.

'Welcome to Madurai, city of nectar,' said the guide. 'According to legend, nectar from Siva's locks fell here…'

He droned on about the history, architecture and religious significance of the Minakshi temple. Tabitha could imagine Andrew as a tiger taking a break. Sitting back on his haunches, he was lowering himself down on to his stomach by shifting his weight from one forearm to the other. He was watching her now as she took photos – of gopurams from unusual angles, elephants as they stroked the heads of devotees, and mahouts having their palms crossed with silver.

The local guide set off on a tour of the temple.

In Tabitha's imaginings, Andrew was thinking about his first trip to India, which he was discovering all alone, the hard way, just after his mother had died. By contrast, Tabitha had discovered India the easy way, in the good company of a group led by a guide following an itinerary. She'd come to appreciate the Indian temple in all its infinite complexity. That said, while the guide was leading them round, she spotted a pink and green handbag made from woven plastic.

'How much?' she said to the stallholder.

'Four hundred rupees,' he said.

'I'll have that,' she said. She scurried to catch up with the group. Andrew took her to one side.

Tabitha thought she was going to be reprimanded, but for once he didn't scorn her shopaholic tendencies. 'Come this way,' he said. 'I've got something I want to show you. It's in the north gallery of the pillared cloisters of the Tank of the Golden Lotus.'

They walked there in silence and Andrew pointed to a rendered blank wall.

'A great loss,' he said, looking as if he was biting back the tears. 'Behind the blank render, there's an exquisite mural depicting the seventy-four miracles said to have been performed by Siva.'

Tabitha turned her head away.

Slowly, Andrew took her chin in his hand and turned her head back to face him. Gently, he stroked her cheek. His fingers are soft, thought Tabitha, and they smiled at each other.

The encounter made Tabitha feel as if she was walking on air.

Down the hallway, Tabitha saw Henry standing by an inscription in marble of the Tamil book of ethics.

'I'm copying it out,' he called.

'All one thousand, three hundred and thirty couplets?' said Andrew.

'All one thousand, three hundred and thirty couplets,' said Henry.

'You had better get on,' said Andrew.

'This spirituality could all be bunkum,' said Tabitha.

Neither Andrew nor Henry responded.

'Have you looked at the ceiling?' said Andrew after a moment.

'No,' said Tabitha. 'I was looking at the cleaners and their brushes. Have you seen the amount of dust they're generating? Not to mention the spider webs they're disturbing.'

Andrew smiled, looked up to the ceiling and pointed. 'The marriage of Minakshi and Siva.'

Tabitha blushed, because whenever there was mention of marriage she thought it referred to her future. 'Isn't it exquisite?' she said.

'One of the most beautiful murals I've ever seen,' said Andrew.

'Purples, greens, yellows and browns, but no reds or blues,' she said.

'How observant you are, my dear Nor Jahaan,' said Andrew.

Tabitha loved it when Andrew called her that. He seemed about to take her chin in his hand again, so she checked that Henry wasn't looking. He wasn't, and Andrew did indeed stroke her chin again. It was heavenly.

Back in the shop, their group was sitting in bamboo chairs arranged around the walls of a room full of carpets, sipping very sweet black Indian tea from bone china cups. Tabitha joined them just as Eric said that he and Tracey were going to be moving to a house that was part of a meditating community. Tracey looked at the pile of carpets in front of her.

'Aren't there any more?' she asked.

'But of course, memsahib, if you'd like to come this way,' said one of the shopkeepers.

'Don't you think we've seen enough for one day?' said Eric.

'No,' said Tracey, and she followed the shopkeeper.

Tabitha looked for her purse. The only thing was, she'd run out of money.

'I am sorry but I couldn't borrow some money, could I?' she said to Gloria.

'But of course, darling girl. How much would you like?'

Out in the street, the heat hit Tabitha like a wall. Identifying a suitable hawker, she went up to him and purchased a fan made from peacock feathers.

Back on the bus, Tabitha admired her new fan and thought of the way in which Andrew had taken her chin in his hand and stroked her cheek softly, not once but twice. It was a pleasant journey.

At the hotel they had lunch. Andrew and Gloria were discussing myth. Tabitha would have liked to join in, but Lévi-Strauss's argument evaded her until after lunch when she was lying on her sun lounger.

'This afternoon I'm going to visit a jungly shrine on the outskirts of town. Does anybody want to come with me?' said Andrew.

'I'll go,' said Rhonda.

'Me too,' said Tabitha.

Andrew hailed a taxi. They passed by wooden and corrugated iron shacks, and telegraph poles from which sagging wires radiated.

When Tabitha couldn't bear the silence any more, she said, 'Would you like to live in India, Andrew?'

Andrew appeared to ponder the matter, then he said, 'I might be interested in spending ten months or so working on a photographic project.'

Oh, what a joy, thought Tabitha, imagining them on honeymoon with their Pentaxes.

There was another awkward silence. To be honest, their visit to the jungle shrine couldn't have come soon enough. Inside the jungly shrine were higgledy-piggledy buildings; some contained shrines, others just rubbish.

'Namaste.'

Tabitha jumped out of her skin. A man, who looked like a caretaker, and his assistant came round the corner. The assistant was bearing a giant garland of marigolds. Tabitha bowed her head and he adorned her.

'Come this way,' said the caretaker. Inside the inner sanctum, he dipped his finger into a large pile of bright yellow powder and anointed Tabitha in the middle of her forehead. He did the same with a red powder and another yellow powder, giving her a tricoloured bindi.

'Now follow me,' he said.

In the corner of the jungly shrine they came to the base of a banyan tree, where the stench of rotten eggs reached its zenith.

'They're for the unmanifest snake,' said the caretaker.

'An unmanifest snake needs food?' said Tabitha.

Andrew and Rhonda joined her.

'But of course, if it's to manifest,' he said.

In the breeze, a mixture of dead leaves and empty crisp packets turned circles. At the thought of the unmanifest snake manifesting, Tabitha felt sick.

'You're looking a bit pale,' said Andrew. 'Perhaps we should go for a tea.'

They took another taxi. This time they were going to a roadside shack, where the sun was setting behind power lines and people were either riding or pushing their bicycles home.

'Three chais,' said Andrew.

Tabitha offered to pay but Andrew declined. It was the first time he'd treated her, and she savoured the moment, sipping her tea as delicately as she could given the dryness of her lips and the thickness of the polystyrene cup.

'How are you feeling?' said Rhonda.

Tabitha was taken aback by Rhonda's display of interest in her. 'Better,' said Tabitha, before asking Andrew who built the Minakshi temple and when.

'Would you like to see where they lived?'

'Yes,' said Rhonda.

Tabitha would have liked to as well. Not knowing about the history of these places was contributing to her increasing sense of disorientation and beginning to do her head in.

Andrew hailed a cab.

'To the palace,' he said to the driver.

'It'll probably be shut,' said the driver.

'This is India,' said Andrew.

The driver smiled.

Tabitha would have liked him to answer her question about the history, but he hadn't. The sky turned deep blue and, as the fluorescent lights flickered on, it got dark. They pulled up in front of two wrought-iron gates supported on two enormous Doric columns that were illuminated by giant spotlights covered in moths.

'It's still open,' said the driver.

'Looks like there might be one of those sound and light festivals going on,' said Andrew. 'I'll see if I can get some tickets.'

After a short while Andrew came back with three tickets, and they entered the main courtyard of the building surrounded by huge Doric columns. To one side was a block of wooden chairs, and they took their seats for the show, which began. The only thing was, they were being eaten alive by mosquitoes. When they could bear it no longer, they returned to the Taj Retreat, where Tabitha took a shower and changed for dinner. On the way to the dining room, she came across a bookseller and bought a copy of the *Upanishads* and a copy of the *Kama Sutra*.

During the course of the afternoon, the group had been divided. As a result, there was much news to exchange and the conversation at dinner was lively.

'I've been to a fabric shop,' said Gloria.

'I've been looking at carpets,' said Tracey.

'I spent the afternoon on the back of a Harley-Davidson,' said Kathleen.

'What did you buy?' said Tracey to Gloria.

'Curtain fabric for my new home,' said Gloria, flapping her big ears.

'New home?' said Tracey.

'Yes, in the Forest of Dean. We're going to be running it as a B&B.'

'I bought a carpet that goes with the decor of our new home,' said Tracey. 'My husband nearly died when he found out how much it was, especially after he bought me that pendant.'

'What pendant was that?' said Kathleen, ruffling her feathers.

'The ruby and diamond one that was in a display case at the Shalimar Spice Garden Hotel. It was our anniversary.'

'I spent the afternoon being driven around Madurai on the back of a Harley-Davidson,' said Kathleen.

'I hope you were wearing a helmet,' said Tracey.

'I was quite safe being driven by one of Babaji's cousins,' said Kathleen.

Tracey didn't comment. Tabitha could hardly believe her ears. When she had said she was going to a wedding, all hell was let loose; when Kathleen got driven off by one of Babaji's cousins on the back of a Harley-Davidson, nothing was said. Tabitha mentioned the discrepancy to Geraldine.

'You went off with unknown tribespeople. Kathleen went off with Babaji's cousins – family, in other words. There's a difference,' said Geraldine. 'By the way,' she continued, 'I noticed you're looking a bit tired. Would you like a sleeping pill?'

Tabitha had never taken a sleeping pill before.

'Yes please,' she said. She couldn't wait to take it. Unfortunately, the effects were not as immediate as she had hoped they might be.

CHAPTER 16

The next morning, after meditating, Tabitha surveyed her corner of the room. As well as a 1950s dressing table and stool with a black leather seat and splayed legs, there was her stuff. It was strewn all over the place and she thought it must be her way of marking her territory. Quick as greased lightning, she packed, removing all evidence of her recent stay just like that.

On her way into breakfast, she took a detour via the pool. In the cool of early morning, the water was still. At the bottom there were blue and white tiles. Beyond the pool there was a row of plane trees with bark like camouflage and green leaves yellowing to brown. Between the trees, hammocks were suspended on thick rope tied with big knots. The hammocks sagged. Later in the day they would be stretched taut under the bottoms of tourists seeking shade. Tabitha's stomach rumbled. She left the pool and entered the dining room. Kathleen was dunking a toasted finger into the soft yolk of a boiled egg. Tabitha got scrambled egg on toast from the buffet and joined her.

'Did you sleep?' asked Kathleen.

'I took a sleeping pill,' said Tabitha.

'I saw you at the wedding,' said Kathleen. Yes, thought

Tabitha, inveigling your way into my territory.

'Are you looking forward to our visit to Tanjore?' said Tabitha.

'Ah,' said Kathleen, 'the capital of the great Chola Empire from the tenth to the fourteenth century that did so much to shape the culture of southern India.'

Tabitha raised her eyebrows.

'Didn't expect me to be so well informed, did you?' continued Kathleen.

'No, to be quite honest, I didn't,' said Tabitha.

'Only joking. It's just that I overheard Andrew.'

On the bus, Andrew told the animals it was going to be a long haul with lots of local interest to see out of the window but that they would be stopping at regular intervals. There was booing. Tabitha kept quiet. She didn't want to make life any more difficult for Andrew, especially not midway through the tour when, in her view, disaffection rates were at their highest.

The bus made its first stop. In bored anticipation of yet another shrine, Tabitha got off. Although a pitchfork and a row of loosely stacked hayricks in a crumbling red barn could have been a Constable, she didn't take a photo. Back on the bus, she castigated herself. It must be the Libra in me, all that emotional indecision. If only I'd been born Aries – all that fire, she thought. She wondered what star sign Andrew was.

'If you look to your left in the middle of the field, you'll see Ayyanar, the riderless horse, homage to an invisible god who patrols and protects villages by night. If you like, you can get off and have a look,' Andrew announced.

There was a group sigh from everyone except Rhonda and Tabitha, who followed Andrew off the bus like puppy dogs. The parched landscape that surrounded them was white-hot. The horse, with its red-rimmed eyes, flowing mane and legs akimbo, looked like it had been spun off a merry-go-round into the countryside.

'Bas reliefs of Parvati, Siva and Vishnu are repeated around the base of the statue,' said Andrew.

Tabitha calculated the number of times. 'Ten times,' she said.

Rhonda counted each one individually and looked at Tabitha in disbelief.

As the bus made its way through small villages, leaving trails of white dust, Tabitha felt as if they were imposing themselves on the villagers, who stood on their doorsteps and stared up at them. At least the houses were white and there were white patterns on their doorsteps.

They got lost. Then when they did finally arrive at the next shrine, there was only a small track edged by a breeze-block wall leading out of the village. Rusted netting sat on top of the wall, and beside it were a fig tree, brambles and swathes of golden grass. Tabitha picked a blackberry. If it wasn't for the heat, we could be in England on a fine autumn day, she thought. The track took them through a field of stubble to a colourful arch.

'Talk about gaudy,' said Geraldine.

'Look at the panels,' said Tabitha. The panels were on the blue columns and were in-filled with red and white floral wallpaper. There were the gods – Parvati, Siva and Vishnu – on a yellow background. Tabitha got out her Pentax and, from behind, took a photo of her companions walking through the arch. Rhonda was wearing her navy-blue salwar kameez and had a bright green rucksack. The hoolocks, Henry and Leticia, were matching in canvas sun hats, white collarless shirts, beige chinos and sensible leather sandals. Geraldine was wearing a floppy cotton sun hat embroidered with flowers, a tie-dye brown and orange smock top, a pair of turquoise linen trousers and comfortable leather sandals. Two locals stood under a tree. On the other side of the arch, the track narrowed to a path strewn with straw and bounded by rows of variously sized sections of upright drainpipe. From the top of each drainpipe, a sculpted horse head projected.

'There's been a mass decapitation,' said Tabitha.

'Most disturbing,' said Gloria.

'I feel as if I'm being watched,' said Tabitha.

'That's because you are being watched,' said Gloria. 'On the other side of those trees there's a goatherd.' The goatherd scampered away.

'Must be weird having a group of tourists, who are actually a bunch of animals, visiting a shrine that is usually the sole preserve of your goats,' said Tabitha.

A smile spread across Gloria's face. Tabitha followed her gaze. It was fixed upon the sculpted red-tipped penis of an enormous sculpted elephant.

In the shade of a huge banyan tree was the shrine itself, a small black figurine of a man with a moustache wearing a turban and a pair of earrings in the shape of a bunch of grapes. In the centre of his forehead there was a red bindi, at his feet the inevitable mixture of dead flowers, ghee, congealed milk and rotten eggs. Gloria sat down on one of the roots of the banyan tree and flicked open her hat.

'That's clever,' said Tabitha.

'It's like a fan,' said Gloria. 'Doesn't get squashed and takes up no space at all, unlike ordinary hats. I got it a long time ago in Indonesia.'

Tabitha was just getting back on the bus when an elderly beggar woman approached. Tabitha only had large notes. 'Next time I come out, I will have small notes and coins,' she said to herself.

The bus set off and Tabitha's tummy rumbled, so when, after a relatively short while, they stopped outside a restaurant with neon signs, she was glad. They descended. Front-of-house staff ushered them through the main body of the restaurant, which was awash with locals, and into a room with two long rectangular tables. Tabitha sat down and looked around.

The door through which they had just come swung back and forth and came to a stop, shut. At the top of the door, there was a round window. Through it, Tabitha could see Andrew's bald head and Babaji's curly locks. As she sat down, it looked like they were checking up on them before leaving them to their own devices – abandoning them even. Tabitha would have liked more than ever to be talking to Andrew. The white tiled walls of the room looked like a room in a lunatic asylum.

A waiter placed a jug of water and a banana leaf on the table. Was Tabitha supposed to clean the banana leaf with the water, she wondered? In the absence of cutlery, the medics among them were the first to wash their hands at a sink in the corner. Tabitha followed suit and cleaned the banana leaf with the water from the jug. The water from it trickled onto her thigh. Waiters dolloped spoonfuls of pureed food the colour of putty on her banana leaf, and Tabitha worried that the food would dissolve into the water and trickle down her thigh too. They were served small metal bowls of rice and then, after their main course, there was a slice of millionaire's shortbread and paan or betel nut wrapped in the leaf of a betel nut vine, which Tabitha mistook for a hot green flannel.

In the lobby of the Parisutham Hotel, Tabitha sat with Gloria, Geraldine and Rhonda on sofas upholstered in a dark blue and white floral fabric. Tabitha picked up the *Hindi Times*. The hotel manager approached with a scrap of paper on which he had written the cost of a single room and a double room. Tabitha wondered why he hadn't just done as he was asked and allocated them a triple room. Gloria rummaged through her handbag for a pencil. On another scrap of paper, she wrote: 'If you're happy to share with Geraldine for the rest of the trip then I'm happy to share with Rhonda.'

Tabitha nodded her head in agreement.

'Would you be happy to share with me, Rhonda?' said Gloria.

'Andrew's allocated me my own room,' said Rhonda and she trotted off, presumably to it. Gloria suggested that they measure up to see if they could all fit into one room.

'Good idea,' said Tabitha, before having yet another rant about the unfairness of the situation.

'When you've quite finished,' said Gloria, 'we can go and measure up.'

They measured the room and went back to the lobby. Andrew and Geraldine were in the middle of a conversation. They turned to Tabitha and Gloria, and Andrew announced: 'From here on in, Rhonda and Geraldine will have separate rooms. Gloria and Tabitha will share, and the extra cost will be borne by Geraldine.'

Gloria and Tabitha looked at one another. Both of them sighed with relief and they all went to their rooms to freshen up before emerging poolside for a much-needed cup of tea. In the middle of the pool there was an island with a date palm that Tabitha swam to. Her head felt as if it was filled with cotton wool. Must be the tiredness, she thought. She needed a break, but she could still hear Geraldine and the hoolocks, Henry and Leticia, chattering away about whether or not they actually existed.

'Testing,' said Babaji into a microphone. There was a high-pitched tone followed by a muffled roar before he passed the microphone to Andrew.

'I think there's been some confusion. We're going to the main temple in Tanjore tomorrow. Today we're visiting a ghat, a place on the riverbank where pilgrims come to bathe, the Ranganathaswami temple, where forty-five thousand people live and work, and an ashram, before coming back to the hotel for some late afternoon tea.'

They were having a pit stop. Tracey and Kathleen were standing by the bus, having a conversation about their respective jewellery. An elderly woman begged them for money. They turned away. How mean, thought Tabitha, giving the elderly woman some money.

At the entrance to the ghat there was a low-arched building, strewn with litter and stinking of urine, which led through to a huge banyan tree. Pilgrims sitting in the shade were having their faces painted. In the distance, the river snaked across the landscape like a glistening black viper. Tabitha took some photos.

She slipped off her shoes and paid the supplement at the temple entrance that allowed her to take photos. Andrew handed them over to a local guide, who took them through a series of disorienting passages until they got to a twisting staircase. At the top there was a viewpoint covered in a pink and white striped awning, like a christening cake. They were dragged so quickly that by the time they got to the inner sanctum Tabitha had got a cricked neck from all the looking back at shopping opportunities. Andrew was staring at something that looked like the top of a giant egg covered in foil. Tabitha noticed his piercingly blue eyes. Then she looked at the giant egg.

'The central shrine can only be entered by Hindus,' said the guide. 'The shrine represents Brahma, the absolute infinite all-pervading consciousness floating effortlessly in the horizontal plane above the teeming, heaving, mad universe. Around the central shrine you'll see seven different temples built by successive Chola, Pandya and Vijayanagara kings between the fourteenth and the seventeenth centuries, each one designed to outdo its predecessor but always preserving the central shrine as is.'

It sounded a bit exclusive to Tabitha – Especially as you can only become a Hindu by birth, she thought – but getting some sense of the history of it all appealed to her ego and made her feel much less disoriented.

Inside the temple, where as non-Hindus they could go, there was an enormous statue of Garuda, the man–bird hybrid, Vishnu's messenger and the courageous bringer of speech. Like a wise old owl he was standing at ease, one claw projecting from beneath a giant sari edged with marigolds, and looking down at them. The buffalo prostrated themselves. Garuda, with his peaceful presence, was yet more evidence of an all-pervading consciousness that manifested in various forms according to the machinations of the human imagination.

The local guide then led them into the hall of a thousand pillars. Henry started counting them but was interrupted by his wife, Leticia.

'Now I'll have to start all over again,' he said testily.

In Tabitha's experience, quarrelling couples were best left to their own devices. Tabitha crossed a courtyard into another hall. Above them, exquisite sculptures were juxtaposed with dangling wires, bare concrete and scaffolding. Nothing like the National Trust, she thought.

'How many pillars did you count?' Tabitha asked Henry, who followed.

'Seven hundred and fifty,' he said.

All of a sudden there was a loud 'Whoopoo-whoopoo' from Leticia – 'whoopoo-whoopoo' being the cry that hoolocks make.

'It's her sensitive feet,' said Henry. 'I'll have to go back and carry her across the courtyard.'

What a romantic gesture, thought Tabitha. Tears came to her eyes.

When it was time to leave, there were so many hawkers to avoid that Tabitha felt like a salmon making its way upriver to spawn, ducking and diving.

On the way to the ashram they got lost, but Andrew was determined and they eventually got there. A high wire fence ran along the perimeter. They followed it round and drove in through the main gate and along a road bordered on either side by concrete edging. Halfway along, Geraldine nudged Gloria.

'Look sharp,' she said, 'to your right – two o'clock – the man in the flowerbed.' She turned round and looked at Tabitha. 'Could be the man for you.'

The man in question was repeatedly hitting the dry stony earth with his spade and, as far as Tabitha could see, trying to dig up a rose. He wore an orange loincloth – bulges in all the right places – woolly socks and heavy work boots. He also had a muscular well-tanned body and a smooth hairless torso, and little golden curls like miniature corkscrews all over his legs, especially his thighs.

'Thank you so much for having my romantic interests at heart,' said Tabitha. I've got other fish to fry, she thought, taking out the clip from her flyaway bun, redoing it and descending from the bus, eyes downcast. She didn't want any potential lover thinking she was anything other than demure.

A slight European woman with dark hair, wearing a diaphanous white salwar kameez, came out from a red-shuttered low cream building to greet them.

Andrew and the woman conjoined their hands in front of their chests and bowed. 'Namaste,' they said.

Then the woman said, 'I'm Valerie. *Enchanté.*'

'The pleasure's mine,' said Andrew.

'I am sorry,' she said, 'but our holy man, or avatar, is not available to meet with you today.' Valerie started to sob.

Andrew put his arm round her.

'Where is he?' he asked.

'In prison,' she sobbed. 'He was wrongly accused of rape and murder.'

'I am sorry. It must be very difficult for you running this ashram all on your own,' said Andrew.

Valerie pulled herself together. 'Please,' she said, 'follow me,' and she led them along narrow red concrete paths edged with marigolds to a communal hall.

In the dining room there were rows of little wooden chairs arranged along the walls and, in front of them, long trestle tables. The animals sat themselves down before being served rice and an assortment of curries. Tabitha could see a kitchen full of stainless steel appliances and surfaces.

'It's disgusting,' said Eric, who was sitting next to her.

'What's disgusting?' said Tabitha.

'Making us all sit in this place where thousands of children could have been abused.'

After lunch, Valerie announced a tour of the grounds would be led by her Swiss-German volunteer colleague, Heinz. Geraldine nudged Gloria and winked at Tabitha.

Heinz was indeed the man who they'd seen digging in the garden.

'My name is Heinz,' he said with a strong Swiss-German accent, and set off quickly.

Geraldine nudged Gloria again and winked at Tabitha.

Tabitha winked back. Like so many horticulturalists who have trained in cold climates, Heinz needed to move fast to keep warm. The animals ran to catch up. Eventually, Heinz stopped under the shade of a frangipani tree.

'Frangipani, *plumeria*…?' he asked.

All eyes fell on Tabitha. She hadn't a clue what the Latin name for frangipani was, so she looked at the floor. Then she looked at Andrew. They had bumped into each other under the shade of a frangipani tree and she was wondering if he remembered.

'*Acutifolia*,' said Heinz.

On the way back to Tanjore, Tabitha fell soundly asleep in the bus. When she woke up, she was hot and sweaty. As only she would, she thought she might have malaria.

After dinner at the hotel – more rice and curry – Gloria, Geraldine, the hoolocks, Henry and Leticia, and Tabitha retired to the crazily paved terrace.

'Kathleen tells me she can hop,' said Tabitha. 'You'd never guess.'

'And you believed her,' said Henry.

'Why wouldn't I?' said Tabitha.

An awkward silence fell. Did Gloria, Geraldine and the hoolocks know something about hopping that Tabitha didn't?

'We're not real,' said Geraldine.

'Yes we are,' said Tabitha.

'No we're not,' said Geraldine and Henry.

'Time for bed,' said Gloria.

'Not if we're not real,' said Tabitha.

All the same, she retired to her bed. If her fellow meditators didn't want to believe that Kathleen could hop, then so be it. She didn't know what to believe any more. Her journey of inner transformation, begun on Elephant Island, appeared to be faltering. Why? she wondered. Maybe the visit to the ashram had put her off a love of all things Indian? Was the avatar guilty of rape and murder? Were the children abused? At the Sri Muthappan temple, the beautiful women and the money changing hands had disturbed Tabitha. She had resolved then to ask Andrew about that but had forgotten – or it could be she just didn't dare?

CHAPTER 17

The next morning, Tabitha identified the chair she wanted to eat her breakfast in. It had a black leather seat and a shiny metal frame in the shape of an 'S'. But when she sat down she found there was no cutlery, and moved one along. Gloria returned from the buffet with a steaming pot of coffee and sat down in the chair Tabitha had just vacated. The hazards of buffet-style eating, thought Tabitha.

'Andrew was just here,' said Gloria.

Tabitha poured herself some coffee and stared out of the window. Andrew was briefing the driver in the car park.

'I hope they're agreeing the route,' said Tabitha.

'Had enough of getting lost?' said Gloria.

'Too right,' said Tabitha.

The driver was wagging his head from side to side. Andrew appeared to have finished his conversation with the bus driver and was coming back in. Tabitha popped her last samosa into her mouth whole, pushed back her chair and got up. She was timing her exit of the dining room to coincide with Andrew's re-entry into the hotel. With any luck their paths would cross in the lobby.

It worked. Andrew smiled at Tabitha, placed his hands on her shoulders and kissed her on the lips. He looked deeply into her eyes.

'My Nor Jahaan,' he said. As Tabitha hit the stairs, she broke into a run and reached their room in record time. She shut the door behind her, leaned against it and pinched herself. Could it really be true that Andrew had kissed her?

She looked in the mirror. She applied some eyeliner, mascara and blusher as well as redoing her flyaway bun. This time not a hair was out of place. She took the stairs down to the lobby two at a time. On the landing she passed Geraldine. Geraldine looked at Tabitha as if to say, Something about you has changed.

Andrew has kissed me, Tabitha wanted to say.

'Tanjore's main temple, known locally as the big temple, has been designated as a World Heritage archaeological site. Note the large granite blocks the colour of the sandstone, the superb statues of Siva, Vishnu and Durga, and South India's largest lingam,' said Andrew.

When they arrived, Tabitha waited in the shadow of one of two gopurams for the resident elephant to anoint her fellow group members.

Andrew said, 'Would you like a ride on an elephant?'

'Could I?'

'You, my proud empress, can do anything you like.'

The elephant was kneeling down.

'Here,' said the mahout. He patted the elephant's thigh. 'Put your left back leg here.'

Tabitha touched her watch on her left wrist to check she was putting the correct back leg on the elephant's thigh. Then she vaulted up on to the elephant's back. Nothing had prepared her for landing on an elephant's back. The expanse of wrinkled grey skin was infinite, or so it seemed. To stabilise herself, she wiggled her bottom. No such luck. Being astride an elephant was like being astride a low hill. The mahout pointed to a piece of orange string tied around the elephant's neck. Tabitha grabbed it. The elephant got up. The view of the temple was magnificent. The elephant ambled. Its stride was long. They went through the second gopuram into the temple courtyard, which was virtually empty of people. They came to a shrine, the statue of a huge bull under an awning.

'What a big bull,' said Tabitha.

'Nandi,' corrected the mahout.

They turned around and came back through the second gopuram. Tabitha heard the sound of cameras clicking, and smiled. They came to a halt. The elephant bent its hind legs, then its forelegs. Tabitha slid backwards then forwards. For a moment, the elephant was still. Tabitha slid into the arms of the mahout. He carried her back down to earth. Smiling, she took a bow and found her Merrells, performance over.

Andrew handed over to a local guide. As he always does thought Tabitha.

'The bull, or Nandi, is Siva's vehicle,' he said. 'According to legend, the Tanjore Nandi was hewn out of a single block of granite. When the bull got too big, threatening the temple, a nail was driven through its back. Visitors to the temple often touch its testicles because its key attributes are strength and virility.'

The local guide went on to ask them why the temple visitor sheds his or her shoes.

'As a mark of respect,' said Tabitha.

'Correct,' said the local guide.

'How did the temple builders manage to install a dome made from a single block of granite weighing over eighty tonnes?'

'By building a ramp,' said Tabitha.

'Yes,' said the local guide. 'The ramp was over six kilometres long.'

The talk over, the animals were free to roam. Tabitha headed straight for South India's largest lingam. Alongside it were rows of smaller lingams. There was also a big black box speaker mounted on a giant music stand from which 'Ommmm' emanated.

In the bus, Tabitha reapplied her make-up and sneezed loudly. Somebody once told her that tigresses who sneeze loudly had big orgasms. She sneezed again.

Andrew looked up. Maybe he was told the same thing, she thought. Here's hoping.

'I hope you're not sickening for something,' said Gloria.

'Me too,' said Tabitha, thinking about malaria again.

In a thatched building with open sides, they watched a demonstration of the lost wax method of bronze casting. For some strange reason, Tabitha couldn't stop thinking of the rhythm method of birth control.

'Wax is much more flexible than clay in that it can be melted down and used again,' said the local guide.

They went next door into a dark mud hut, where women were decorating wood with precious stones and making papier mâché. The glue was made from a mixture of flour, water and turmeric and mixed in coconut half-shells. Tabitha spied two paintings on glass. One was of Brahma supine, creating the universe. The other was of Lakshmi afloat on a lotus leaf.

'How much?' she asked.

'Six hundred and fifty,' said the salesman.

'I'll take those,' she said. The salesman wrapped each painting in a sheet of white tissue paper. Carrying them carefully, Tabitha made her way to the bus.

'What have you got there?' said Andrew.

'Would you like to see?' she said.

'Yes please,' said Andrew. Tabitha unwrapped the paintings and showed him.

'You have done well,' he said. Tabitha smiled and licked her lips, pleased as punch.

At lunch, there was silence among the group. It was awkward. Tabitha couldn't bear it any longer, so she went to the pool where it was hot and busy, not a deckchair in sight. The side of the pool was curved like the crest of a wave. Tabitha lay on it with one hind leg dangling in the pool and the other on the crazily paved terrace surrounding the pool. She tried to relax, but it was hard when she might have burned at any moment and, worse still, she might have missed the trip to the museum.

At reception they were out of change, so the beggars would have to wait.

In the lobby of the museum, Tabitha was trying to rotate a white plastic postcard stand. It wouldn't budge, so she looked through it to see what the sticking point might be. Rhonda was on the other side. No wonder it won't rotate from my side, thought Tabitha.

Tabitha walked into the first of the museum's galleries.

'I once brought a group of water diviners here. In the ninth and tenth centuries, the sculptors used to bless the stone before using it. In so doing, they set up energy fields that can still be detected today,' Andrew informed them.

'Were these sculptures made using the lost wax method?' said Tabitha.

'No, these sculptures are made from stone,' said Andrew, slowly enunciating each word.

Tabitha realised her mistake and felt stupid. Something about being on tour seemed to rob her of all of her faculties, she thought.

'The bronzes are in the next room.'

In the gallery, Andrew beckoned Tabitha over.

'These statues demonstrate the Indian ability to accommodate contradiction,' he said. 'They're androgynous, timeless, ageless, dynamic, static – all of these things and more.'

'Look at the pinches of skin behind the knee,' said Tabitha.

'The detail is incredible,' he said.

'The wrinkles around the tummy button.'

'That bulging stomach.'

'The way distortions in reality are seamlessly accommodated.'

'Say more,' said Andrew.

'Look at the multiple arms and legs emanating from that torso as if it were entirely normal.'

'I must remember that.'

Tabitha was pleased as punch. Again she licked her lips.

She and Andrew parted company, then they reconvened.

'This one's special,' he said, looking at a statue of Parvati. 'Siva's consort holding the entire universe in the empty space between her forefinger and her thumb.'

Tabitha thought of a saying – something she'd been wanting to tell a lover for some time. It went as follows: I honour that place in you where the entire universe resides, where if you are in that place in you and I am in that place in me, then we are one. But, in relation to Andrew, she held back.

'I could use this statue as a basis for a garden design,' she said.

'Say more,' said Andrew.

'Her fingers could be a five-bar gate, her arm, a path edged with holly…'

'Hold it in mind for the future.'

She and Andrew parted company. Tabitha did her own whistle-stop tour of the remainder of the galleries. Then she went outside into the peppermint-green courtyard. She spotted an interesting doorway. Inside, there was a staircase. At the top there was a whale skeleton.

The bison, Eric and Tracey, were standing in the aisle of the bus with their forearms resting on the seat backs. Tabitha squeezed past them and took up her normal position, seated one row from the back on the left-hand side.

Hearing a *vrmmmm, vrmmmm*, they all looked round. Kathleen, without a helmet, was fast disappearing on the back of a motorbike. It must belong to one of Babaji's relations, thought Tabitha.

'Next time we see her will be in rehab,' said Tracey.

'So irresponsible,' said Eric.

Their next expedition was to a silk factory. A short journey by bus, then a walk past tiny mud huts brought them to a pedestrianised zone. Up ahead, Tabitha could see a bundle of white threads stretched between two trestles. When she got closer, she realised they were silk. Babaji herded the animals into the front parlour of one of the tiny huts. It was a bit of a squash – there was a loom, two women weaving strands of iridescent blue silk thread, Andrew and Babaji, as well as the animals.

The next hut was more like a warren. The animals made their way down a small corridor into a parlour where they sat on white plastic chairs. In a small recess halfway up the wall, there was a red flashing statue of Siva, welcoming them or warning them – Tabitha couldn't tell. On the floor, the inhabitants of this hut, who were attentive to their every need, laid out saris. Tabitha's favourite had a checked red and yellow pattern. Gloria picked it up and Tabitha panicked lest Gloria bought it. Then, when the prices were revealed – well over eighty pounds and well outside Tabitha's budget – she relaxed. Gloria put the one she had chosen back. So did Clodagh and Rhonda. Tabitha felt bad because the locals had gone to so much trouble. Luckily, Tracey saved the day by buying a bright green one. She also took a couple back for Kathleen to see.

The sun was setting red. It was balmy. Sitting on a white plastic chair under a palm tree, Tabitha's legs were aching and she could have done with a glass of white wine. To hell with the expense, she thought.

At dinner, back at the hotel, the animals were sitting on the same crazily paved terrace as last night. Eric, to Tabitha's left, yawned.

'I hope I'm not boring you,' said Tabitha.

'Not at all,' said Eric, and then he did an enormous wolf whistle.

Gloria, Geraldine, Rhonda, Leticia, Tracey and Clodagh – all the female animals bar the tigress – were descending the steps, all dressed up in saris and salwar kameezes. If it weren't for the facts that they were all animals and they weren't wearing sashes, they could have been in a Miss India beauty pageant. Tabitha tried not to laugh.

'You know something?' said Eric.

'No,' said Tabitha.

'You could pass for thirty – thirty-five at most.'

'That's very kind of you to say so.'

'And you know something else?'

'No,' said Tabitha.

'If I were a little younger, I might have tried my luck with you.'

'What about your wife?'

Tabitha could sense Tracey staring daggers at them.

'Well, put it this way. If I were a little younger and footloose, I'd have tried my luck with you.'

'Would you indeed?'

'Why did you come?'

'I'll tell you one day...'

'Why not now?'

'I don't feel like it.'

'If not now, when?'

'Maybe on the last day of the tour.' Pushing back her chair, Tabitha took leave of the group.

'Going so early,' said Callum.

'Places to go, people to see...'

'As in?'

'Clubbing downtown with my boyfriend.'

'Don't you want to see the dancing girls?'

Gloria was standing in reception.

'We're leaving first thing in the morning, so I thought it as well to settle up now,' she said.

'Good thinking,' said Tabitha.

Andrew and Babaji were at the other end of the counter looking at Andrew's photos. Tabitha would have liked to be looking at Andrew's photos with Andrew, but she wasn't. Too bad, she thought, but she wouldn't want him to see hers, so she understood – hers were too bad.

CHAPTER 18

Next day, on the bus, Andrew sneezed again and again.

Multiple orgasms, thought Tabitha. Either that or he's got a cold.

'Time for one of Andrew's little sleeping pills,' said Babaji.

'Today,' said Andrew, 'we're heading north-east to the Chidambaram temple, one of Tamil Nadu's most holy sites. Here we will be attending the Rudra Abishekam puja. This is a precise set of actions made all the more powerful by the fact that they've been repeated in exactly the same way since the sixth century. The temple is run by high-caste Brahmins called Dikshitars, who marry within their caste and support themselves by asking local people for alms. In return for the alms, the Dikshitars make offerings at the temple, send local people the resulting ash and invite them to special feasts. Ritual of this kind is sorely lacking in the West. Take the example of the outpouring of grief at Princess Diana's funeral as a demonstration of the need for a new world order based on a merger between Western rationality and Eastern spirituality. A need that has never been greater.'

'Anyone for chai?' said Babaji. The bus stopped halfway to the Chidambaram temple and Tabitha made her way to the front.

'You're looking flushed. Are you all right?' asked Babaji.

'Never been better,' said Tabitha. 'That was a fantastic sleeping pill. Have you ever addressed it to a wider audience?'

'No, but then I've never been complimented like that,' said Andrew, taking both Tabitha's cheeks between his forefingers and thumbs and squeezing them big time. From behind, Gloria cleared her throat, then, as if she were her chaperone, she shuffled Tabitha out of the bus and along to the chai stall.

'Would you like a cup of tea?' Tabitha asked her.

'Yes please,' she said.

Tabitha got two cups of very hot tea in polystyrene cups. The tea burned her tongue. But this was no break.

'Come along now,' said Babaji to the group. 'Andrew's going to deliver yet another of his little sleeping pills.'

'The temple you can now see is known locally as the Nataraja Temple and is dedicated to Siva.'

'Not him again,' muttered Tabitha.

'Was that something you wanted to share with the group, Nor Jahaan?'

'No,' she muttered, blushing.

'The temple was built by Hiranya Varna Chakravarti, who had leprosy and came to Chidambaram on a pilgrimage from Kashmir in AD 500.'

'A bit like Babaji,' Tabitha piped up.

'Not exactly, Nor Jahaan,' said Andrew. 'After bathing in the temple tank, reputedly he was cured. If you'd like to follow me, we're going to enter the temple through the oldest, Eastern gopuram, which was built in AD 1250. Once we're inside, we'll go straight to the chit sabha, or hall of wisdom, where Siva is worshipped.' The group proceeded, Andrew in the lead, Babaji bringing up the rear.

They came to an open-sided building with a tiled roof supported on four columns and with a floor about a metre higher than ground level. A Dikshitar directed them to proceed along the side of the building until they came to the foot of a small flight of stone steps.

'Wait,' said the Dikshitar. Then he whispered something into Andrew's ear and, all of a sudden, all the males in their party started taking off their shirts. Tabitha's eyes nearly popped out of their sockets. Andrew's chalky-white chest was in stark contrast to the sunburn on his neck and his arms.

'Cat got your tongue?' said Gloria.

Andrew was climbing the mounting block. Tabitha watched him go, especially his chalky-white chest. On closer inspection, she could see the odd grey hair and flaking skin, but they didn't put her off.

'Ladies,' said the Dikshitar, inviting the female animals to climb the steps.

When they were all gathered at the top, Andrew told them they were going to witness the lustration of a lingam. 'We don't want to miss it,' he went on. 'I've already made one donation too many to the Dikshitars.'

'Typical Scot,' said Tabitha.

'What was that?' said Andrew.

'Nothing,' said Tabitha.

Tabitha had had enough of other individuals. She withdrew from the conversation and, insofar as she could in a small building, one half of which had been cordoned off, made herself scarce. Finding a black metal pillar to lean against, she stared into one section behind a burgundy velvet curtain and another behind a portcullis. Tourists and devotees piled into the building, making her feel even more overwhelmed. There were bells pealing, pigeons flying and Dikshitars running around carrying oil lamps which burned with swirling black smoke.

'It's where the lingam is prepared,' said an unfamiliar voice behind her. Tabitha turned round. A local man with a smooth brown chest and a burgundy sarong tied round his waist was pointing to the section behind the curtain.

'I see,' said Tabitha.

'It won't be long now before they perform the lustration. If you keep your eyes peeled and watch it, you'll be cleansed.'

He must be a temple guide, she thought. Slipping in front of her, he clung to the portcullis. Tabitha watched small drops of sweat run in rivulets from the nape of his neck to the base of his spine. She imagined them moistening the crack between his buttocks. She could feel her own beads of sweat running down her spine. When they got to her coccyx, they dropped to God knew where. She didn't like to think.

A young man now popped out from behind the curtain and there was a hush. Tabitha's heart pounded in her throat. The young man drew back the curtain and the rings scraped on the pole. One got caught on some dried bay leaves and the devotee struggled to free the curtain. Another man helped him and, as they freed up the curtain together, bay leaves flew up into the air.

Tabitha saw the lingam first through heads with black hair. For a clear, multi-faceted crystal, no more than three inches high, boy, did it have presence. The two men were joined by others who continually splashed the lingam with water. Like mercury, the water split into myriad droplets. Tabitha's heart slowed and she felt cooler. The lingam was placed on a small burgundy velvet cushion with yellow tassels at the corners.

'Keep your eyes on the lingam. They're going to make an offering to Siva,' said Tabitha's personal local guide.

She tried to maintain her gaze on it, but the flame of an oil lamp to the left of the lingam distracted her. She could see Nataraja – Siva in his form as a dancer – dancing in the flame. Bumping her head on the metal pillar, she turned round. A cradle, strung on a cotton thread and tied to the metal pillar, rocked. She prayed – for her next lover, for a cub and that she might find her place in the world.

'How do you account for the different-sized lingams?' said Tabitha at lunch, trying to fill yet another of the empty silences of which they seemed to be having more and more.

'Good question,' said Andrew, 'to which I'm afraid I don't know the answer.'

'What about the different sounds associated with different lingams?' asked Tabitha.

'Again, another good question to which I don't know the answer,' said Andrew.

Tabitha hoped he was a better lover than anthropologist.

'We had better get going,' he said. 'Our next haul is to Pondicherry and it's a long way.'

The next thing Tabitha knew, after a long sleep, they were pulling up outside the Hotel D'Orient. Seagulls were screeching and there was sea air and sunshine, and blue sky to boot. Tabitha may not have been able to see the waves but she could see the light reflected from their surfaces dancing in the street. The kerb, marked with a white line, was high. She took a big step down from the pavement and grabbed her small green bag from among the suitcases being unloaded from the bus. The white walls of the Hotel D'Orient abutted the street. Tabitha looked up. High windows, centrally pivoted with long dangling cords, were open to the world. She climbed the steps to the front door. On either side there were columns. Inside was a double-height hall, more columns, a panelled ceiling, a floor tiled with narrow zigzag black and white tiles, an antique reception desk and a palm in an old terracotta pot. Tabitha's black pointed suede slip-ons went clickety-clack on the floor like a stag's hooves on stone. On the far side of a courtyard there was a bar, where steam rose from an ice bucket and the barman polished glasses with a white damask cloth. He turned each glass to the light and scrutinised it for blemishes before polishing it again.

Tabitha sat down on the raised edge of a fishpond in the courtyard and eyed the goldfish. Iridescent orange bodies flicked paler tails as they scooted for cover in brown silt between the knotted roots of green-stemmed papyrus.

Andrew sidled up beside her.

'You're in room seven with Gloria,' he said. 'Have you seen her?'

'I'm over here,' Gloria piped up. She was on the far side of the fishpond and could be seen through the wispy umbrella-shaped tops of the papyrus.

'Would you like to go up now?' said Tabitha.

'Shall we?' said Gloria.

Porters wearing billowing white cotton shirts over black silk pantaloons with burgundy cummerbunds and pointed red silk slippers, and carrying the elephant's suitcases, appeared as if from nowhere. They climbed up tiled stairs, the treads edged with worn wood. The walls were uneven, with flaking white paint. The landing, when they got there, was open to the courtyard. The porter turned to the left, and ahead of them he threw open two tall slender doors.

Gloria and Tabitha took deep breaths. At the centre of the room were two single four-poster beds. The porter went into the room and put down Gloria's suitcases.

'Anything else I can do for you, memsahibs?' he said.

'Not at the moment,' said Gloria.

He bowed. 'Namaste,' he said.

'Namaste,' said Gloria and Tabitha, bowing.

They looked at one another.

'In the interests of maintaining personal space,' said Tabitha, 'I think we should pull our beds apart.'

Gloria laughed and they pulled the beds apart. Gloria unpacked and then lay on her bed. Tabitha explored. Beyond the beds there was an area separated from the bedroom by two half-height walls, one on either side. Behind one there was a loo and a bidet; behind the other there was a shower.

'What are the bathroom arrangements like?' said Gloria.

'Put it this way,' said Tabitha. 'If we were lovers they would have been perfect.'

'I get it,' said Gloria, laughing.

The bed was higher than normal, and Tabitha had to haul herself up. The bedheads were decorated with carvings of gods and goddesses doing God only knew what, and inset with tiny mirrors which sparkled in the light.

Tabitha thought about Andrew at lunch: his hand as it had moved slowly up her thigh. She remembered his embrace in the car park and his kiss in the lobby. Much as she admired his intellect, she wanted his pasty white body with its flaky white skin and sunburnt arms. More than anything, she wanted his passion. She wanted his hand gently caressing the inside of her thigh.

All of a sudden they heard great guffaws of laughter.

'What's that?' said Gloria.

'Sounds like it's coming from the hoolocks' room,' said Tabitha.

'Let's go and see what's going on,' said Gloria.

They left their room and headed in the direction of the laughter. The door to room five was open. Even so, Tabitha knocked.

'Come in,' said Henry. The hoolocks and Geraldine were sitting on the highest bed Tabitha had ever seen – so high that there was even a set of steps with handrail, pommel and landing stage.

'Come on up,' said Henry.

Gloria climbed the steps and got onto the bed with the hoolocks and Geraldine. Their legs were dangling over the edge. There was a lot more giggling. Tabitha wished she could have joined them, but she felt too inhibited.

Back in their room, Tabitha perused the bookcase and came across *The Rough Guide to India*. She looked in the index. The section on Pondicherry began on page 112, but unfortunately page 112 and the subsequent pages were missing. She heard the sound of footsteps. The door opened.

'Another beautiful room,' said Andrew.

'Isn't it just,' said Tabitha.

'Would you like to have a look at mine?'

'Yes please. Gloria is currently visiting the hoolocks but I'll be along with her as soon as she gets back,' said Tabitha, looking down demurely.

'I'm down the passageway on the left-hand side.'

'See you soon.'

Gloria returned to their room and they set off for Andrew's.

'Come in,' he called when Tabitha knocked.

Andrew's room was distinctly masculine, with a low, wide bed and a low, wide cane chair. Tabitha imagined the various love-making positions they could adopt on both. Andrew was staring right past her at Gloria, who was still outside the room.

'Mind if we join you?' she said.

'Not at all,' said Andrew. Gloria, followed by the hoolocks and Geraldine, entered the room. There was lots of oohing and aahing, then Tabitha left.

Back in their room, she looked at her watch. It was four o'clock. Tea was optional and dinner was at seven. Time for some exploring, she thought.

Two blocks away from the hotel, Tabitha joined the local people promenading. To her right was a string of higgledy-piggledy rocks and a dark blue sea with white horses, to her left a run of terraced houses that could have been in Brighton. In the distance, she could see an enormous bronze statue. She assumed it was of Gandhi but needed to go and check.

She hadn't gone very far when she met Kathleen, the bison,

Tracey and Eric, and the buffalo, Callum and Clodagh.

'Out for some air, are we?' said Eric.

'Yes,' said Tabitha. Just when I thought I'd got away, she thought.

She changed direction and headed in one block from the sea. Here, outside a fruit stall, she bumped into Gloria, who was perusing the merchandise. Tabitha continued on in the direction of the statue, passing a white stucco house with slender white columns, set in a manicured park. The ornamental beds were in geometric patterns. There was a sign to the Hotel Du Ville and another big house painted grey. Its windows were barred. Tabitha peered inside. She could see bespectacled men with short-sleeved shirts filing large piles of paperwork. Indian bureaucracy at work.

When Tabitha felt sure that she wouldn't bump into anybody else that she knew, she headed back to the promenade. The statue towered over her. She looked at the plaque: Gandhi, all right. She continued along the promenade until the hard surface began to disintegrate. Then she followed a rough road to a fishing community where, in between dilapidated wooden shacks, there were small pebble beaches. Brown water and flotsam ebbed and flowed, rose and fell. Spume flew in the breeze. Rabid-looking dogs nosed for scraps in among tin cans with sharp edges. Tabitha winced.

'Boat trips to see dolphins!' cried the fishermen. Nothing would have given Tabitha greater pleasure than to have communed with dolphins. She looked at her watch, but there was no time.

Eventually she came to her kind of beach: white-crusted sand, upturned fishing boats made from hollowed palm trunks, blue sea. She was tempted to take a plunge but there were too many people around. Instead, she perched her behind on one of the upturned fishing boats. Children with sweet smiles, mostly young girls, gathered around her. They were frightened at first.

'Where are you from?'

'London,' said Tabitha.

'London, England?'

'That's right. Now teach me some Tamil.'

Between them, they taught her the Tamil for eyes, nose, mouth, ear and chin.

Then Tabitha offered them coins. They refused.

'Would you have preferred pens?' she said.

'Buttons,' they said.

Tabitha was puzzled. They each mimed the act of ironing.

Now Tabitha got it. Because the irons were heavy, the buttons came off their clothing. Tabitha pressed coins into their little hands and walked away to the back of the beach.

Her feet sank through the hard crust on the top of the sand as if it were icing on top of a cake. Behind the beach there was a triangle of open sea grass, where a group of young boys were playing cricket. Tabitha had seen countless other boys playing cricket on this tour. No wonder the Indians were so good at it.

Sauntering back, she found herself in a cul-de-sac. At the end, there was a brightly coloured tent. Outside the tent, she sat down on a white plastic chair and was offered a cup of chai by a woman in a sophisticated sari. She'd happened upon a funeral party. She didn't want to impose or get sucked in, as she had with the wedding, so she reversed out of the cul-de-sac and came across an antiques shop.

In she went, thinking, This would please Andrew. She picked her way through wood carvings, glass, ceramics and paintings, all covered in an unbelievable amount of dust. She chose the things Andrew would like and put them to one side. Then she took the proprietor's card. If Andrew wanted to come and have a look he could do so, though how he would get any of the stuff home God alone knew.

Finally Tabitha arrived at a clothes boutique. She passed her paws over the rails and came across a royal blue dancer's outfit embroidered with silver. She tried it on. Looking in the mirror, she imagined herself in it later that evening, entering the dining room. Andrew and the others would applaud. Tabitha would curtsey and smile. Her royal blue dancer's outfit would float in the balmy breeze.

All of a sudden her wits returned. She looked in the mirror again and saw a sweaty older tigress looking most peculiar in a blue dancer's outfit. What had she been thinking?

Tabitha peeled off the royal blue dancer's outfit embroidered with silver and put it back on its hanger. Next she tried on a long, collarless black cotton shirt. This is much more my ticket, she thought, elegant and understated. As she paid for it, she thanked God her sanity had returned. What a fool she would have made of herself. She had wanted to pander to Andrew and his love of all things Indian. He seemed to have such a sway over her. But it was time to wake up to who she truly was.

Tabitha slipped back into the hotel room.

'Is that my long-lost spiritual ballast come to save me?' said Gloria.

What a really lovely thing to say, thought Tabitha.

'Shall we meditate?' she asked.

For dinner, she changed into her new black top and wore it over a pair of pale green cotton Cut Loose trousers embroidered with a floral design. When she made her entry into the dining room, nobody even looked up. She coughed.

'Is that a new top I see?' said Kathleen.

'Yes,' said Tabitha.

'Give us a twirl,' said Kathleen.

Tabitha did as she was told. Andrew pulled out a chair for her.

'It's like the top of a salwar kameez,' he said.

'Yes,' said Tabitha, smiling naughtily. 'My sole concession to Indian dress.'

'There's a set menu, so you don't have to choose,' he said.

Breathing a sigh of relief, Tabitha sat down. At their table, the talk was of the internet and travel. Despite having strong views on both, Tabitha couldn't think of anything to say. She would have liked to tell Andrew about the things waiting for him in the antiques shop, but she couldn't summon the courage, and after a while she withdrew to make her way upstairs.

On the landing, there was another bookcase and a bench. Tabitha extracted a book and sat down, thinking Andrew would pass by on his way to bed. She was hoping he would pass by, say that he loved her, and ask her to join him in his room.

All of a sudden, he did appear.

'Are you reading?' he asked.

'Yes,' she said.

He passed on, went to his room and shut the door. Then, shortly after, he reappeared. Tabitha's hopes rose, but he passed by without comment. The footfall of his sandals was near-silent. Tabitha felt like a lemon, to say the least.

CHAPTER 19

'Good morning, darling girl,' said Gloria. 'Here, take my place. I'm just going.'

Tabitha picked up a white linen napkin and smoothed it over her thighs. She was wearing a pair of pale blue trousers. Andrew was sitting opposite her reading the *Hindi Times*. The newspaper had been ironed and its spine was slotted into a piece of wood to stop it from creasing. It had a tassel dangling from one end. On the front cover, there was a photo of a married couple at breakfast and Tabitha imagined Andrew and herself, were they to be married, doing the same. Geraldine was sitting next to Andrew.

'I followed you yesterday,' she said to Tabitha.

Her words filled Tabitha with horror. A tigress being followed by a glang – whatever next?

'I'm not stalking you, if that's what you're thinking. It's just that you were striding out with such confidence, so different from the local women, I wanted to see where it got you.' Geraldine swirled the last of her tea around in her cup, downed it, got up and winked at Tabitha.

'We'll see you two lovely things later on. Come along now, Henry, Leticia, we need to get going.'

Andrew refilled both their coffee cups.

'I saw you struggling at supper last night. It can be difficult to socialise after a puja.'

'I saw Nataraja yesterday.'

'Where?'

'Dancing in the flame.'

'Well, we're going to the ashram this morning, but you'll probably need some time alone.'

Time alone, thought Tabitha. No. What I want is time with you. But she couldn't say that.

'I'll come to the ashram and then I'll see how I feel,' said Tabitha. 'By the way, I have a theory that individuals, human or otherwise, like order.'

'Why do you say that?'

'When I am coming round from a faint...' Andrew frowned. 'Don't worry, I don't do it very often, and I've always done it ever since I was a cub... When I come round, it's like looking out of a train window when the train is travelling at speed, and trying to make sense of it all. The last time I fainted, I was at the acupuncturist's. He was trying to strengthen the element of fire in me.'

'What a coincidence, Nor Jahaan. The Arunachala temple in Tiruvannamali, where we'll be going next, is dedicated to Siva in his form as fire. We'll have to arrange a special puja for you. By the way, what do you do when you're not on tour?'

'Design gardens.'

'Oh yes, that's right, you said. Our reincarnated Sufi who designs gardens – I remember. For the rich and famous, I suppose.'

'As it happens, yes. I was once involved in the redesign of the walled garden at Kensington Palace for Princess Michael of Kent.'

'Were you indeed?'

On the far side of the courtyard, there was a second staircase. Tabitha climbed up and, leaning over the balustrade, she could see that Rhonda, Kathleen, the bison and the buffalo were still having breakfast at another table.

Behind her on the landing, she could hear the hoolocks talking. Their bedroom door was open.

'Hey guys,' she called over the balustrade. 'You've got to come and see the bed in the hoolocks' room.'

'Do you mind?' she said, turning to the hoolocks.

'Not at all,' said Henry.

Rhonda, Kathleen, the bison and the buffalo piled into the hoolocks' room. Eric sat in the corner on a steamer chair, hind legs up in front of him. Rhonda pointed at the set of steps with handrail, pommel and landing stage.

'What are those?' she said.

'For climbing onto the bed,' said Tabitha.

'Oh,' she said.

'Have a go.'

'Can I?'

'Come on up,' said Henry. Rhonda climbed the steps and jumped on to the bed. Everyone else rose slightly as she landed in the centre of the mattress. Thankfully, the bed didn't break.

Gloria and Tabitha gathered with the other animals in reception, ready for the day's activities.

'There are seven rickshaws waiting for you outside,' said Babaji.

In the street the sunlight was bright, and Tabitha squinted. To be honest, she didn't like the idea of being pulled by a horse, but if Babaji was in favour then who was she to query it?

'You can go with Kathleen,' said Babaji to Tabitha. She was disappointed not to be travelling with Andrew, of course. She had hoped to be able to continue their conversation of this morning about her spiritual life.

With Kathleen's big feathery bottom to contend with, there

wasn't much room for Tabitha on the well-worn black leather seat. Once they got going, she realised that travelling by rickshaw with the cover up had a number of advantages. First of all, there was shade. Second, there was rhythm from the clippety-clop of the horse. Third, there was a breeze. Fourth, and best of all, the view was framed by the curve of the cover.

They visited the sites that Tabitha had visited the day before. Then they drove to the Muslim quarter. Here the houses were brightly coloured and had verandas surrounded by bars. On the verandas there were benches. Tabitha took a little nap on one of them. Babaji hurried her along. The first and subsequent storeys of the houses overhung the ground floor. A man wearing a salwar kameez and a tightly fitting cap, and who owned one of the houses, gave them a tour. Tabitha joined at the back. Unfortunately she didn't hear much of what was being said, because Tracey had chosen this time to tell Tabitha about the house she was having built back in Blighty.

Their next stop was the Sri Aurobindo ashram. It was a low grey building with white trim and a red tiled roof. A veranda surrounded a courtyard, which had a tomb at its centre. A long line of devotees snaked its way around the courtyard, presumably waiting in line to pay their respects to Sri Aurobindo.

Gloria and Tabitha sat on the step of the veranda and meditated. Then they needed to pee. They found the loo and waited for an inordinately long time. In the end, Tabitha looked under the door. No legs, animal or otherwise. Next door to the loo, there was a woman arranging lotus flowers and water hyacinths.

'Is there a toilet?' Tabitha asked her.

'You have to go to reception to get the key,' she explained.

Outside the ashram, their rickshaws were waiting.

'Would you like to buy a kola set or a drum?' a street hawker asked them.

'What's a kola?' said Gloria.

'A pattern made on the ground outside a house to ward off evil spirits. Each set is made up of small bags of coloured powder paint and a set of perforated tubes – each one a different pattern. To make a pattern, you put the powder paint in the tube then roll it around on the ground outside your home.'

Gloria and Tabitha bought one kola set each.

They drove to a restaurant, where they had lunch. The restaurant was on the first floor of a building with no ceilings, just rafters open to the roof. Andrew was sitting at one end of a large table. Tabitha was at the other end.

She told her fellow travelling companions about the time she went to Mongolia. 'We were told not to take stones out of the country. My tigress friend Emma put stones in her socks and tried to smuggle them out. She was stopped at customs. "I thought it meant precious stones," she said, smiling sweetly. "No," said the customs man, waving her through. Emma's tigress mother, a doctor, went to a conference in Moscow later that year and told one of her colleagues about Emma's stone smuggling. "You know why?" said the colleague. "The Gobi's where they do the nuclear testing. You're not allowed to take the stones out in case they're radioactive." Emma's tiger father, also a doctor, had a Geiger counter and was able to test the stones. They were safe.'

Tabitha's fellow travelling companions listened open-mouthed and Tabitha felt like the hostess with the mostest helping Andrew entertain his guests. Bodes well for the future, she thought, when Andrew and I will take people and animals on tour together.

Gloria and Tabitha settled themselves into Room 101 of the Ramakrishna Hotel. A strange noise emanated from the bathroom.

'The sink judders,' said Gloria. 'You only have to touch it and it nearly falls off the wall.'

'Thanks for the warning.'

'Shall we go for a recce?'

'Do you mean to the next ashram?'

'Sounds like a plan.'

Outside the hotel, there were lots of small yellow tuk-tuks circling like bees. Their driver didn't ask them where they were going. Tabitha guessed he assumed that, as Westerners, they would be going to the Sri Ramana Maharshi ashram.

Wide, white marble steps marked the entrance to the ashram, which was surrounded by green metal railings. Inside the ashram was a black marble plaque inscribed with an account of how Sri Ramana Maharshi achieved his spiritual awakening aged sixteen and then went to live in caves on the mountain known as Arunachula behind the ashram.

They entered the main hall and sat down to meditate. Tabitha was distracted by all the comings and goings. When she opened her eyes, she saw both Westerners and Indians. She didn't like to generalise but there was a type of Westerner – pasty white, wearing salwar kameezes with Birkenstocks. Their feet were blistered and the women who had babies carried them in slings.

Back at the hotel, Gloria and Tabitha freshened up before eating their dinner, vegetable curry and mango kulfi, at a shiny black Formica table in an airless room with no windows.

'It's an early start tomorrow. We need to be at the main temple for a puja that starts at nine thirty,' said Andrew.

'Am or pm?' Tabitha asked facetiously.

Andrew frowned. Tabitha took it he didn't find her that funny.

'Nine thirty am,' he said firmly.

Gloria, Geraldine, the hoolocks and Tabitha retired to a row of white plastic chairs in the lobby.

'I've had enough of pujas,' said Tabitha.

'Why do they have to be so early?' said Gloria.

'I could do with a lie in,' said Henry.

'Me too,' said Leticia.

All of a sudden, Tabitha got the giggles. So did Gloria and so did the hoolocks. It happened just as Rhonda, Kathleen, the bison and the buffalo came in from the street.

'What on earth's the matter with you?' said Tracey.

'We've had enough of pujas,' said Henry.

'We were just saying the same thing, weren't we, Tracey?' said Clodagh.

Andrew had better watch out or he may have a revolution on his hands, thought Tabitha.

'Have you told Andrew?' said Rhonda.

'No,' said Tabitha.

'We tried to go out clubbing,' said Kathleen, 'but there weren't any clubs.'

'No pavements either,' said Rhonda morosely.

Gloria and Tabitha retired.

'You were naughty making fun of Andrew and his pujas,' said Gloria.

'No harm done.'

'I always feel a tiny bit manipulated by him,' said Gloria.

'Tell me about it,' said Tabitha, recalling her royal blue dancer's outfit and antiques escapades.

'Do you mind if I read for a bit?' said Gloria.

'Not at all. I'm going to write my diary,' said Tabitha.

'It's a bit airless in here.' Gloria opened the window.

Tabitha went into the bathroom. The sink shuddered.

'Be careful of the sink,' said Gloria.

CHAPTER 20

In the morning, Gloria and Tabitha meditated before they went down to breakfast. Gloria chose to sit with Andrew and Babaji. Happy days, thought Tabitha. Getting to be with Andrew without making it obvious I'm interested. What could be better?

'Ready for today's puja?' he asked.

'Most certainly,' said Gloria.

Little bit of a traitor, thought Tabitha, eating banana fritters.

Then, when Gloria stood up, her trousers fell down at the same time.

'Let me help you with those,' said Tabitha, getting the giggles again.

To the right of the hotel entrance, there was a sign saying 'Ladies. Privacy!' Tabitha followed a passageway until she got to a basic loo where, all alone, she defecated. What joy.

Outside, Babaji was gathering tuk-tuks.

'You go in this one,' he said.

Tabitha was so disappointed not to be with Andrew, who hadn't been calling her by her pet name of Nor Jahaan quite as much as she would have liked. She repeated it silently to herself.

When they got to the temple entrance, Tabitha took off her pointed black suede slip-ons. The shoe shelves were chaotic and she feared for their safety. Inside the temple, Andrew was walking at quite a pace. They followed him to some cloisters and sat down on cool granite slabs. Tabitha looked around. Gloria and Kathleen were nowhere to be seen. 'I'll go,' mouthed Tabitha to Andrew.

Retracing her steps, she soon found them, and the relief on their faces when they saw her was palpable. Tabitha returned them to the fold. Andrew looked relieved. Tabitha felt pleased with herself and sat down again cross-legged in the queue, only this time she couldn't get comfortable. Geraldine was sitting between her and Andrew, so he wouldn't see she couldn't adopt the lotus position. Phew, she thought.

'Are you from London?' said one of the local women in the queue.

'Yes,' said Tabitha. The language barrier prevented the conversation from developing.

'I'm sari watching,' said Gloria. 'To see if I can see if any two saris are alike.'

'Not as far as I can see,' said Tabitha.

'This way, memsahibs,' said one of the temple staff, giving them baskets containing eucalyptus leaves. They were funnelled up a small staircase. At the top were two large double doors and, on the threshold, a metal step. They crossed over the metal step into the inner sanctum of the temple. Behind them, the large double doors began to close. It was Tabitha's last chance to escape. It was getting hotter and hotter. She thought she was going to faint.

Lungi-clad, bare-chested, sweaty, pony-tailed priests picked their way through the throng. Some of the animals were standing, others were sitting cross-legged on the floor. At the far end of the inner sanctum, there was the image of Siva in his form as god of fire. The priests disappeared behind it, and when they emerged they were carrying oil lamps, which they lit in front of Siva. They swirled them, trailing black smoke. There was chanting. All of a sudden a clear film of water poured over Tabitha, as if she were in a weir. She'd never known anything like it. As the doors opened and she bounded out into the cool air, she felt clean, refreshed and invigorated as never before.

There were beggars outside and Henry made a donation, so others, wanting the same, set upon him. One, an elderly bare-chested man with stumps for legs, tried with his crutch to trip Henry up. Henry made a getaway. Simultaneously, a shopkeeper beat women and child beggars with a gnarled stick.

Horrified, Gloria and Tabitha got a tuk-tuk back to the hotel.

At lunch Andrew announced, 'The puja is a process of purification.'

'It makes me feel like I do when I've whirled as a dervish,' said Henry.

Tabitha explained how she felt during and after the puja. Andrew nodded and smiled. Tabitha felt as if she'd made some progress on the road to spiritual enlightenment and wanted to talk to Andrew about it in private, so she tarried at the table. But she had no luck. Eventually she left, disappointed, and wandered aimlessly around the hotel looking for the perfect place to write. On a landing underneath the staircase, she found a black leather sofa, where she installed herself and started to write.

Of course, it wasn't long before Rhonda, Kathleen and the bison came by, asking what she was doing.

'Writing,' she said.

'Not about us, I hope,' said Tracey.

Perhaps I will, thought Tabitha.

Gloria and Tabitha got a tuk-tuk to the ashram, where they met Geraldine and the hoolocks, Henry and Leticia. They suggested meditating in the room where Sri Ramana Maharshi said: 'They say I am dying but I am not going away. Where could I go?' The ever-present chanting distracted Tabitha, as did naughty thoughts of shutting her companions into the room. There was a green baize door with a sliding lock on it.

They left the ashram. Geraldine complained about the pollution. She covered her face with a hanky. All of a sudden, Andrew appeared.

'Are you wanting to visit the mountain?' he said.

'Yes,' said Henry, 'but I think we've taken a wrong turn.'

'Follow me,' said Andrew.

They retraced their steps. This time, inside the ashram, they passed by kitchens, bedrooms, outhouses and a herd of cows grazing in a small paddock. Then they climbed a small set of dilapidated concrete steps and went through a rusted gate in a rusted fence. Andrew told them that the path divided up ahead. One path went round the mountain and the other, to the left, went up the mountain.

'I'd suggest you go up the mountain,' he said. 'I've heard some stories that the path going round the mountain is dangerous for tourists.'

Personally, Tabitha would rather have gone round the mountain, but for some strange reason she was prepared to sacrifice her interests in favour of the group. Must be that journey of inner transformation initiated on Elephant Island making me less selfish, she thought.

Gloria, Geraldine, the hoolocks and Tabitha set off. The path got steeper. Gloria started wheezing.

'Are you all right there?' said Tabitha.

'It's only my asthma. Don't worry, I'll be fine.'

This time, Tabitha took Gloria at her word and left her behind. The first cave had a door and a series of interconnected rooms, each one hewn deeper into the rock. Unlike most caves, there was no litter and no smell.

'Shall we meditate?' said Geraldine.

'No, we can't,' said Henry, looking at his watch. 'There's a notice on the door saying that the cave shuts at five.'

Geraldine pointed to a cave further down the mountain. 'What about meditating there?' she said.

There wasn't a path, so they descended by way of a scree slope with boulders and rubbish. Outside the cave, there was a terracotta-tiled terrace shaded by a *Cupressus x leylandii*. Inside, there was a whitewashed room with a wooden bench along one side.

'We can sit here,' said Geraldine.

They came out of the cave an hour or so later, and the town of Tiruvannamalai lay in a haze on the plain below. The sun was setting red in a grey sky. They descended from the mountain, passing by a well, and Tabitha thought it was lucky Rhonda wasn't with them, otherwise she might have done her party trick and fallen down it.

When they got to the bottom of the mountain, they took a tuk-tuk back to the ashram.

'I'm going back to the temple,' said Henry, much to Leticia's consternation.

Tabitha left them to it and went in search of Gloria, who had survived her abandonment. They took another tuk-tuk back to the hotel. The inhabitants of Tiruvannamalai were lighting oil lamps and placing them in the entrances to their homes.

'It must be a very special celebration tonight,' said Gloria.

'Of great spiritual significance to the locals,' said Tabitha.

'It's important to respect the locals,' said Gloria.

'I wonder what I'm going to wear. I had thought of going as I am,' said Tabitha.

'You can't do that,' said Gloria.

When they got back to the hotel, Tabitha changed into a pink and white dress with a floral pattern. She wore it over a little white T-shirt and a pair of bright pink silk trousers.

Tabitha followed Gloria into the dining room and Gloria headed straight for the table that Andrew, Babaji and Geraldine were sitting at. Tabitha ordered vegetable curry.

'Are you coming to the Shivaratri Festival?' said Andrew.

'Yes,' said Tabitha.

A look of impish anticipation spread across Andrew's face.

'So am I,' said Gloria.

'How long will you be spending there?' Geraldine asked.

'I really don't know,' snapped Andrew. 'With such a regimented life, I rarely get to do as I please.'

Geraldine left the table. Tabitha couldn't say she blamed her. Poor Geraldine. Tabitha went in search of her. She found her in the stairwell, sitting on the black leather sofa where Tabitha had done her writing. Geraldine was on the verge of tears.

'I'm sure he didn't mean to snap,' said Tabitha.

'I only wanted to know how long he was going for because I'm feeling very tired.'

'You will come, won't you?'

'I guess so.'

'It's a once in a lifetime opportunity.'

'Oh, all right then.'

'Good. We're going to give you such a good time,' said Tabitha to Geraldine.

'I think you should go in one tuk-tuk with Andrew and we'll follow on behind in another,' said Geraldine.

'I think we should all go in one tuk-tuk,' said Tabitha. She still didn't want anybody thinking she was chasing Andrew, least of all his nibs.

They went down to the lobby and Andrew put in an appearance wearing a white sherwani over a white salwar kameez. He hailed a tuk-tuk. Andrew sat in the front, next to the driver. Geraldine, Gloria and Tabitha piled into the back. Squashed in the middle, in between Gloria and Geraldine, Tabitha didn't rate her chances of seducing anybody at that particular moment, let alone Andrew.

'I can hardly breathe,' said Geraldine, covering her mouth with her shawl. 'The pollution's so bad.'

They stopped outside a small door in the temple wall.

They took their shoes off and Tabitha carried hers in a small red and yellow cotton bag that she had been given by the hotel. The stone beneath her paws was still warm from the heat of the day. On the other side of the door there was a narrow passageway between big granite blocks. Dust had accumulated in the corners between the blocks. Tabitha was reminded of the temples in Egypt where sand from the desert blows into the corners between the blocks.

The passageway led into a courtyard, where they climbed a staircase. At the top, on the terrace, they could look down into the courtyard and see families bedding down for the night, lighting candles in the hope that Siva might pay them a visit.

They descended the stairs.

'Time for me to say goodnight,' said Geraldine.

'Me too,' said Gloria.

'What would you like to do?' said Andrew to Tabitha.

'Provided I'm not cramping your style, I'd like to stay,' she said. She could hardly believe her luck.

'Night night,' said Geraldine and Gloria.

'I hope they'll be able to find their way back,' said Andrew.

'They'll be fine,' said Tabitha.

'This is the highest gopuram in southern India,' he said.

'Sixty-six metres,' said Tabitha.

Andrew looked surprised.

'I read it in the guidebook.'

Andrew smiled and affectionately squeezed Tabitha's cheeks between his forefingers and his thumbs.

'Where would you like to go?' he said.

'Back to the inner sanctum,' she said.

When they got there, a massive procession was moving around the inner sanctum. They joined in. The speed of the procession increased. They withdrew to one side. It was like being in an eddy. There was a cacophony of noise and, in among it, the sweetest sound.

'What's that?' said Tabitha.

'Do you mean the chanting?'

'That's it – the sweetest sound I've ever heard.'

'We are in the hall of a thousand pillars,' said Andrew.

Most of the pillars were black, but some of them had been carved into brightly coloured horses and mythical lions known as vyala.

'It's like a fairground,' said Tabitha.

'You couldn't dream it up if you tried, could you?'

'It's surreal.'

Outside the temple, they ordered two black coffees. The waiters were turning the chairs upside down and placing them on the tables. They sat on a step.

'In places like these I'd like to melt,' said Andrew.

'Look,' said Tabitha. 'The pattern in the lights is of David's star.'

A look of delight danced in Andrew's eyes. Tabitha could hardly contain her passion, so she moved away from the step. Andrew followed. They went back into the temple and moved from shrine to shrine, but it felt as if they danced. In one, there was a black lingam.

'My favourite,' said Andrew.

At Lakshmi's shrine, Tabitha told Andrew this was her favourite.

'Goddess of money and good fortune,' said Andrew. 'What's this?' he said, pointing to a green climber with a tiny white flower.

'Jasmine,' said Tabitha. 'But you don't need to know the name of a plant to make it sing with another.'

'One of your philosophies,' said Andrew.

'Yes,' she said.

They visited the next shrine.

'Where Ramana Maharshi was eaten by rats to no ill effect,' said Andrew.

In a second courtyard they came across a maze that had been laid out in oil lamps. Without getting burned, Tabitha tip-pawed her way to the centre and back.

In yet another, bigger courtyard, they sat down cross-legged and listened to an Indian musician playing the vina.

'There was a shrine near the pool that I'd like to investigate further,' said Tabitha.

'Sure,' said Andrew.

They got to a four-headed lingam set into a yoni. They walked around it. On one side there was a gulley. Andrew sat down on one side of the gulley and Tabitha sat down on the other.

'Come over here,' he said.

Stepping over the gulley, Tabitha made herself comfortable on the ground beside him. He put his arm around her and held her tight. Thank goodness for that, she thought. I haven't misread the signs. Heaving a huge sigh of relief, she put her forearm around his bent knee and kissed it again and again. Then she caressed the fingers of Andrew's left hand. Andrew held his right hand up and pointed to Venus rising, shining brightly in the night sky. Andrew reclined. Tabitha reclined. They canoodled.

All of a sudden there was the sound of a stick tapping on the ground. The tapping got louder. They couldn't ignore it. Looking up, they saw an elderly man wearing a poncho made from a blanket and tied at the waist with a leather belt. He was wielding a wooden staff with prickles and invited them to follow him. They left the temple and entered a bazaar. There was a stall selling tea.

The elderly man took money from the tin he had stowed in his belt and paid for three teas.

'Our new friend looks like Ramana Maharshi,' said Andrew.

'Do you think he did this to stop us canoodling in the temple?' asked Tabitha.

'I've no idea,' said Andrew. 'Is it time to go back to the hotel?'

'Yes please.'

Andrew hailed a tuk-tuk. Tabitha got in first. Andrew followed. They snuggled up in the back seat of the tuk-tuk, all very cosy. He licked the inside of her ear. A shiver ran down her spine and her tummy turned somersaults.

When they got back to the hotel, the dawn was breaking, a sliver of pink light on the horizon.

'I hope we haven't been locked out,' said Andrew.

Tabitha laughed at the thought.

Luckily, the hotel was still open. Andrew and Tabitha climbed the stairs to the first floor. He kissed her. It wasn't as passionate as she would have liked it to be.

'Thank you for a beautiful evening,' said Andrew. Turning, he crept to his bedroom.

In Tabitha's room, Gloria appeared to be in the land of Nod – either that or she was pretending. Getting into bed, Tabitha placed her head on her pillow and fell soundly asleep, foolishly happy in the thought that she'd found her man.

CHAPTER 21

Gloria had left the room. Must be late, thought Tabitha. No time to meditate. Extricating her legs from the tangled sheets, she got out of bed, dressed and bounded down to breakfast. Tabitha entered the dining room through a dark glass door.

'Good morning,' she said.

Slowly, Gloria put down her copy of the *Hindi Times*, removed her pince-nez and took a sip of her coffee. 'Andrew already has a girlfriend,' she said.

'Funny you should say that. Rhonda said as much when we were at the Brunton Boatyard Hotel, only I didn't believe her on account of what Andrew said in the taxi driving from the airport to the Taj President,' said Tabitha.

'And,' said the elephant, 'he's not interested in having cubs.'

Now, that did come as a bit of a blow, as there was nothing Tabitha would have liked more than to have cubs. The waiter came over. He was bearing a platter with a silver doily and three samosas.

'I took the liberty of ordering them for you,' said Gloria.

'Thank you,' said Tabitha.

'In my view, men who don't want children shouldn't get in the way of their animal partners who do. I don't see why their animal partners can't just get on and have cubs, in your case, if they want to,' said Gloria.

Music to my ears, thought Tabitha. At least I will have Gloria's support when I accidentally on purpose fall pregnant with Andrew's first cub. That said, it will be different with me. With me, Andrew will want to have cubs. While she pushed her samosas around her plate, Gloria got up and left.

Alone, Tabitha reflected. The truth of it was finally sinking in. No wonder he hadn't kissed her as passionately as she would have liked last night. He was all partnered up. As far as she was concerned, it was over. Tabitha didn't do men who were spoken for. She thought back to their first meeting – the warmth of his dulcet tones. He'd said he was single, hadn't he? She thought back to the time when he put his hand on her thigh and to the time when he asked her to repeat Kahlil Gibran's definition of love. The pet names he called her, Nor Jahaan and My Proud Empress, then their first embrace and his kiss upon her lips. Out of these threads she had woven a tapestry upon which they might lie. The only thing was, he lied. Tabitha climbed the stairs to the room with a heavy heart and a brave face.

Gloria and Tabitha prepared themselves for the day's activities and took a tuk-tuk to the ashram. To one side of the entrance, there was a bookshop. Tabitha perused the books, but she couldn't seem to concentrate. What she really wanted was for Andrew to come and find her. She imagined him whispering sweet nothings into her ear, telling her how much he wanted to make love to her.

Hope soon turned to grim realisation. In spite of her obvious ability to forgive Andrew, she must take him to task. Delving more deeply into the bookshop, she perched herself on a stool and prepared her speech: 'Not only have you lied to me about being single, you have also, knowingly while in a relationship, led me up the garden, if not the temple, path. To make matters worse, you had no intention of seeing me again, either now, to see how I am, or at any time in the future.'

To her surprise, Andrew rounded the corner of the bookshelves.

'Are you all right?' he demanded tersely.

Tabitha crumpled.

'Fine,' she said, 'just fine. You don't have to worry about me.'

Then she pulled herself together. She was a single tigress; life went on.

Lunch was in a big white hall with high windows. Banana leaves had been laid out on the floor as plates. Local people, chattering away, were using their hands to scoop a creamy white mixture containing diced carrot into their mouths. To be honest, they looked like elephants using their trunks and the creamy mixture looked like sick.

Tabitha got a tuk-tuk back to the hotel and went straight to the room. Over her bikini, she donned a tight purple crop top and a pair of bright orange shorts. She also put on her black suede slip-ons and took a small white towel. She climbed the stairs to the top floor of the hotel. There was a balcony with a small parapet. She leant over. Tiruvannamalai was as frenetic as ever. She thought about jumping, but decided against it.

She spread the small white towel over a white plastic chair and sunbathed. The heat was unbearable. She lasted a quarter of an hour. Then she wrote her diary, recording her feelings for a life she was determined to have even if she didn't know what it was going to be about. At dinner she chose to sit as far away from Andrew as possible.

CHAPTER 22

The next morning, the bus, like an old familiar friend, was waiting. Staff loaded luggage while Andrew, Babaji and the animals hopped aboard.

'Today, we'll be heading north-east to Kanchipuram,' droned Andrew, 'one of India's seven most sacred cities, a place where holy ground gives rise to a field of active power that allows moksha, or spiritual realisation, to take place.' He went on, 'I hope you enjoyed your time in Tiruvannamalai – one of the highlights of the tour, I find. Many of my guests have remarked on the tranquillity of the place.'

Tabitha looked out of the window. Revellers, many of them with oranges and lemons sewn to their chests, were still enjoying themselves in the streets. Nothing tranquil about it, she thought, falling asleep.

'Time for a chai stop.' Andrew was waking Tabitha up, shaking her by the shoulder.

The loos were across the way, in a building that looked like a cross between a mosque and a music hall. To get to them, Tabitha crossed a big room. There was a rusty bed. She wanted to cry.

She sat down on a wooden bench at a cafe back on the same side of the road as the bus.

'Would you like a cup of tea?' said Andrew.

'Yes please,' said Tabitha. To be honest she hadn't expected Andrew to be so attentive to her needs so soon after the demise of their relationship. It felt nice that he was running around after her. And, of course, he didn't know that their relationship had ended.

They pulled up outside the hotel Baboo Soorya at 85 East Raja Street. Tabitha extricated her small green bag from the luggage pile by the side of the road, and she and Gloria made their way to room 212 via an antiquated lift.

'At least the air conditioning works,' said Tabitha.

She and Gloria unpacked in the cool, then it was downstairs to the dining room for a light lunch.

'As well as being renowned for its spiritual qualities, Kanchi is also renowned for its silks,' announced Andrew. 'This afternoon, we're going to pay a visit to BM Silks, House of High Fancy in the Gandhi Road near Rangasamy Kulam.'

When they got there, there was a sign above the door: 'Celebrated saris since 1976'. Inside, silks of every colour were piled high to the roof. Salesmen stood to attention behind counters. As soon as they saw the animals, silks appeared to take off, unfurl in mid-air and, as if piloted, land perfectly displayed on counters. At the centre of the room there was a column, surrounded at its base by a bench upholstered in dusky pink velveteen edged with tassels. Tabitha sat on the bench. Andrew joined her. Her tummy churned. Hope sprang eternal.

'Traditions should continue if they work, if they continue to be of use to the people who practise them,' said Tabitha anthropologically.

Andrew smiled and nodded; she imagined it was because he agreed with her.

Babaji was herding the other animals towards the exit.

'If anybody wants to buy anything else, they had better get a move on,' he said.

Tabitha had thought this was her day for not shopping, but she was tempted by two pieces of silk. One was mauve shot with pink and the other was brown shot with red. They were both embroidered with gold. In the back room, she got out her credit card and paid.

Andrew and Tabitha left the shop together. With their bags – Andrew had also indulged – they looked like a couple making a guest sitcom appearance on *Absolutely Fabulous*. All of a sudden there was a screech of brakes and a thud. A motorcycle had hit Geraldine. It wasn't serious, and the glang dusted herself down.

'You should look where you're going, young man,' she said.

'So should you,' said the young man.

'Really,' said Tracey.

Andrew walked over to the scene.

'You've cut your knee,' he said. 'Babaji, will you get a plaster from the first aid kit in the bus?'

Babaji obliged and Andrew applied the plaster.

'An accident waiting to happen,' said Eric.

'Are you all right?' said Clodagh.

'I think so,' said Geraldine.

'Here, let me help you to the bus,' said Clodagh.

Gloria and Tabitha retired to their room. Tabitha reclined on her bed and admired her new silks.

'What on earth am I going to do with them?' she said.

'You could give them to your friend who's been looking after Twinkle and the kittens,' said Gloria.

What a good idea, thought Tabitha.

'Would you mind if I had a shower?' she said.

She blow-dried her fur just as she liked it to be and applied a thin line of black eyeliner. Some lines of what could be a poem came to her:

'I've sat with you on temple step,
Imagined lights reflecting there,
Seen patterns in the darkened air,
Of David's star…'

She ran out of steam. Anyway, she didn't want to be late for their visit to the Shankaracharya of the South. Gloria, looking lovely in her paisley shirt and grey pleated skirt, her hair swept back into a chignon, hurried Tabitha along.

On the bus, Andrew told them they'd be visiting the Hindi equivalent of the Archbishop of Canterbury, in a complex of buildings known as the Kanchi Kamakoti Peetham. The bus driver parked in a cul-de-sac. Andrew led them along the sides of two courtyards. The second was filled with exotic plants. They went into an office with old filing cabinets and a typewriter, where they waited while Andrew was called away.

When he came back, he told them that they'd been granted an audience with the Shankara of the South at seven thirty the following morning. It was a great honour, for which Tabitha was extremely grateful.

On their way out, the Shankara, surrounded by his colleagues, passed them by. When he smiled, Tabitha could see that he had a missing tooth, and she warmed to him. There was a holy ceremony underway in the ashram and the chanting was sweet.

'You look like you've received darshan,' said Andrew.

'What's darshan?' said Tabitha.

'The sighting of a god,' said Andrew.

The butterflies in her stomach flapped their wings.

*

When they got back to the hotel, Andrew called Tabitha to him and away from the group that was going up to bed. 'Nor Jahaan,' he said, 'you really are extraordinarily beautiful.'

'Thank you,' said Tabitha.

Their eyes met. That was all, but she returned to Gloria and Geraldine on cloud nine.

Tabitha couldn't sleep for thinking about Andrew, the compliment he'd paid her and those piercing blue eyes. She thought about slinking out of her bed, along the corridor and into his bedroom. Then somehow or other she managed to fall asleep. In her dreams, she was an insect with long legs that meant she could go anywhere, including Andrew's bed.

CHAPTER 23

It was seven thirty on the dot. Gloria, Geraldine, Kathleen, Rhonda, the hoolocks, Henry and Leticia, and Tabitha had arrived at the Shankara of the South's ashram. They were shown into a room next door to the room where they had waited the day before. It was furnished with a glass-fronted wooden bookcase, a filing cabinet, a table and a chair. As well as the animals, there were some local devotees. They all sat on the floor and waited for the Shankara. In due course he came in, dragging one of his feet and wielding a roughly-hewn wooden stick. An entourage surrounded him. He sat down on the chair. He spoke either Tamil or Hindi and his words were translated into English.

'Welcome,' he said.

'Your holiness,' said Andrew, 'some of our group belong to a meditation society whose former head sought spiritual guidance from your holiness's colleague, the Shankara of the North. If you wouldn't mind, they'd like to ask you a few questions.'

Henry said, 'We've spent much of our time over the past three weeks discussing the question of whether or not free will exists. Might his holiness like to contribute to the discussion?'

They waited while the question was translated.

In Tabitha's view, this took some time because free will was a Western concept.

'But of course it does,' said the translator at last.

'Are you sure?' said Henry.

'You decide what to do, whether or not to have children, how many to have,' said the translator impatiently, mirroring the Shankara's tone.

Kathleen, the devout Catholic amongst them, looked shocked. 'Are you sure there is free will?' she said.

Henry was about to speak again. Time to butt in, thought Tabitha – if we're not to appear rude, that is. 'If you were able to identify the single most important message that you were trying to get across in your work here, what would it be?' she said.

'Find the Para-atman, or the Universal Self, in yourself, recognise the Para-atman in others and do service,' said the translator.

A mobile rang. One of his holiness's entourage passed him the phone.

Tabitha couldn't understand what he was saying but imagined he was resolving some dispute or other. While he was still on the phone, a gaggle of local devotees gathered at the window asking for darshan. Still on the phone, the Shankara obliged. Talk about multitasking.

They got up from various positions, some cross-legged on the floor. Passing her hand over her bottom, Tabitha aimed to dislodge any dirt that had accumulated there.

'Thank you,' she said to his holiness before bowing and leaving the room with the other animals.

'Feel free to wander,' said Andrew. Tabitha went in search of the chanters she'd heard the day before. To no avail. Instead, she found two calves. One was a cow's and the other was an elephant's. Both were decorated with daisies.

*

When they got back to the hotel, Eric asked Tabitha, 'Seeing as you now have a direct line to Andrew, could you suggest to him that we leave this dastardly hotel as soon as possible?'

'I'll see what I can do. No promises,' said Tabitha.

She found Andrew. 'The bison and the buffalo are desperate to leave this establishment,' she said.

'I refer you and them to our original itinerary,' said Andrew tersely.

Tabitha reported back to the bison and the buffalo and regretted her interference.

As she got on the bus, she apologised to Andrew. He didn't reply.

'We're nearing the end of our journey. Just one final haul south to Mahabalipuram,' he announced.

He's oblivious to the needs of others, thought Tabitha. And she asked Geraldine for one of her spiritual books.

'Of course – which one would you like?'

'You choose.'

Geraldine handed Tabitha one of her books. Tabitha read it cover to cover. At the end, she discovered that she understood more about the concept 'I have nothing of my own; therefore I have everything'. It didn't just apply to things, it also applied to people, including Andrew. She didn't need or want him. She fell asleep.

When she woke up, she felt as if she had been in a very deep sleep. She looked out of the window. She could see a very long way. All of a sudden, it was as if the earth moved. Like a slide clicking into place, her sight became clearer; the lines were sharp, the colours bright – sharper and brighter than she had ever known. The bus came to a halt. Her reverie came to an end. Handing the book back to Geraldine, she descended from the bus.

She hadn't taken any photos since she'd had her first batch developed. To be honest, she was a bit disappointed with them. Now it felt good to be taking photos again, and she took several of women harvesting wheat.

They turned into a drive.

'We're just arriving at our last stop,' said Andrew, 'the Ideal Beach Resort.'

The grounds were extensive. Many of the plants, which Tabitha didn't recognise, had rings of soil surrounding them to conserve water and were painted white to prevent insects from attacking them.

In the distance, through a haze of pink tamarisk, Tabitha could see a patch of blue sea. She breathed in the salt air. Check-in could wait. She bounded down a crazily paved path to the back of the beach, where there was a rusted kissing gate. On the other side, her feet sank into the warm sand and she stared at the waves. If ever there was a choice between nature and culture, give her nature any day of the week. To be honest, she was all templed out.

The other animals were sitting on the terrace sipping welcoming cocktails, and Andrew was dangling their key.

'I can't wait to swim,' said Tabitha. 'This place is gorgeous.'

'You deserve it, my dear Nor Jahaan,' said Andrew.

Gloria and Tabitha went to their chalet. Whipping out a turquoise sarong with fish on it, Tabitha grabbed a towel and her Ambre Solaire and headed for the beach. The waves broke over her head as she swam and there was a strong undertow, which made the water a murky green. Gloria, Geraldine and the hoolocks, Henry and Leticia, joined her.

'It's not exactly a swimming pool,' shouted Henry.

'You've been corrupted – too many luxury hotels,' said Tabitha. She toyed with the idea of pretending she was a shark, but even she wouldn't be so dastardly. She emerged from the water, skin tingling, and spread her towel on the beach. Then she lay down and applied Ambre Solaire so that she could soak up the sun with gay abandon. She was in love with this beach.

After dinner Tabitha joined Rhonda, Kathleen, the bison and the buffalo in comfy chairs near the bar.

'I don't feel I've talked to you since you first had the kittens,' said Callum. 'How are they and would you like a drink?'

'They're fine and I'd love a vodka tonic,' said Tabitha.

'Just the kind of drink I'd expect a tigress like you to drink,' said Tracey.

When the tigress's drink arrived with ice and lemon, it had condensation running down the sides. Her fingers were wet when Andrew came out on to the terrace. Callum offered Andrew a drink.

'No, thank you,' said Andrew. 'I'm going for a walk. I haven't yet had a chance to see the sea.' And with that, he disappeared.

Tabitha sucked on her lemon, extracting every last drop of alcohol in which to drown her sorrows. She also ate the ice cubes.

One by one the others left the bar – all except for Kathleen.

'I've had such problems with the laundry service in the various hotels we've stayed in. The clothes always seem to come out pink,' she said.

This, then, was Tabitha's fate: to listen to Kathleen's complaints about her laundry.

Much to Tabitha's surprise, only ten minutes later Andrew returned from the beach.

Again he refused a drink, but this time he stayed.

'I'm off to Bedfordshire,' said Kathleen.

'Night night,' said Tabitha. She turned to him. 'How are you feeling?'

'Tired,' he said, 'but…would you like to go for a walk?'

Tabitha nodded.

They walked together along the crazily paved path and passed through the kissing gate. Andrew kicked off his sandals.

Tabitha slipped off her slip-ons, which quite literally flew through the air.

'Your wizard shoes,' said Andrew, taking her paw. He slipped his arm around her waist and drew her towards him. 'I've been resisting this moment with every sinew and bone of my body.'

Tabitha slid her arm around his waist and drew him towards her. Their hot bodies melded with one another briefly. And then he led her down the beach.

The lights from the hotel faded into the indigo dark all around them. At first the incline of the beach was steep, then it lessened and Andrew selected a flat spot. They lay down and gazed up at the pale moon, partly veiled by cloud. The stars were bright. The moon's light was reflected in the sea, a pale path to a darkened horizon.

'Why did you say that you were having to fight this with every sinew and bone of your body?' asked Tabitha, sitting up.

'Because I haven't been entirely truthful with you,' he said.

'Go on,' she said.

'I'm still in a relationship...albeit a disintegrating one. And as a guide on tour I have a rule not to get involved with any of the women who travel with me.'

'I knew you were in a relationship,' she said.

'Intuitively?'

'No, Rhonda and Gloria told me,' she said.

'When did you first know?' said Andrew.

'Know what?' she said.

'That you loved me,' said Andrew.

'I don't know,' she said. 'What about you?'

'As soon as I saw your postcard,' said Andrew.

'The one of my garden?'

'Jungle, more like,' said Andrew.

'I know,' she said.

Tabitha told Andrew the story of how she was at a luncheon party with her friend John in the countryside when Hermione, who wasn't able to come on tour because she'd had a stroke, told her about the tour. Hermione said that a man called Andrew Wynter-Blythe was leading it. 'I had just bought your book.'

'What a coincidence,' said Andrew.

'That's what I thought,' said Tabitha.

'In spite of your independence, I'm sure you want children,' said Andrew.

'Just one, and an orphan,' said Tabitha. She'd always dreamed of having one cub of her own and an orphan. Now her dreams were about to become a reality – or so she fondly thought.

Andrew smiled and drew her towards him.

She was just about to nuzzle his chest when he placed his hand on her cheek and turned her face to his. He kissed her. His kiss was the softest kiss she'd ever known. Also, he kissed her passionately with his whole mouth. This time there was no holding back. She responded, kissing him passionately with her whole mouth. As their passion built, she felt for his penis. He moved away from her and disappeared into a bush at the back of the beach. She heard him pee. Then he came back and took her in his arms again. They kissed, and again she felt for his penis.

He pulled away. 'What's before us is a sacred act,' he said, getting up.

He led her back towards the hotel then. The sand underfoot was still warm from the heat of the day. The breeze was gentle. Palms stirred. They swung each other's hands.

When they got to the kissing gate, he said, 'What puzzles me is why you aren't already shacked up?'

'I guess it's because I haven't found the right man,' she said.

'Until now,' said Andrew as they reached the kissing gate.

Tabitha had to hold the gate for support.

On the other side, Andrew told her he was having difficulty dealing with Geraldine.

'She has just lost her husband,' said the tigress, encouraging him to be more compassionate.

They parted company shortly after that and she went back to the room she was sharing with Gloria. Again Gloria was either asleep or pretending to be. Whatever, Tabitha got into bed and tried to sleep.

CHAPTER 24

'Today we're visiting Mahabalipuram, the last temple of the tour,' said Andrew. 'The Pallava kings experimented with temple design by instructing their craftsmen to build miniature versions of proposed temples.'

Tabitha took some photos of the miniature temples and then they went to another site, where they climbed a flight of stairs hewn from the rock. At the top, to left and right, there were two friezes, also hewn from the rock.

One was of Durga, Siva's wife, in her furious form, riding on a tiger and slaying the demon buffalo. The other was of Mahishasura and Vishnu lying under Adishesha, the seven-headed serpent, effortlessly creating the universe from stillness.

'I only have enough photographic film to photograph one or the other,' said Tabitha.

'Durga represents the feminine,' said Andrew, 'the other the masculine. Take your choice…'

'I'll go for Durga,' said Tabitha. Andrew took a photo of her, then of some teenage boys larking around in front of Durga's image. She envied him his abundance of photographic film, and also wished he would kiss her some more.

'Which one do you prefer?' said Andrew to the male buffalo.

'I haven't decided,' said Callum. Callum's new-found interest in art was impressive, and towards the end of the tour. Must be the Andrew effect this time encouraging animals – in particular, buffalo – to share in his love of all things Indian, thought Tabitha. Funny, though, how the male buffalo chose to express it in front of Andrew and me rather than his wife or the bison.

At the foot of the steps there was a huge banyan tree with a poster on the trunk.

'What does it mean?' Tabitha asked the group of teenage boys, who were still larking around.

'It's encouraging people to use condoms,' said one of the boys.

The others giggled. Tabitha wished she hadn't asked.

Chip, chip, chip, went the stonemason's chisels on stone. Everywhere, the air was filled with a fine grey dust. At the roadside she fondled an apple carved from jade. She couldn't resist it, so she acquired it for a few hundred rupees. The skin of the apple was smooth. The stalk, where it had broken off from the tree, was rough. She took it to represent the break from the tree of life.

'What's that you've got there?' said Andrew. She showed him. He smiled.

'For lunch you can either go back to the hotel or I've booked a table at a local restaurant.'

'I'll come with you to the restaurant,' said Gloria.

'So will I,' said Geraldine, the hoolocks, Henry and Leticia, and Tabitha. The restaurant had overhead fans, peach-coloured walls, a white marble floor and dark green ferns in terracotta pots. Their table was small and rectangular. It was also made from white marble and had white metal legs.

'I wonder what the weather's been like at home,' said Gloria.

'I spoke to my son,' said Eric. 'He said there'd been snow.'

The conversation turned from the weather to the congestion charge.

'I think schemes based on fining people for bad behaviour are based on unsound principles. If I were prime minister for just one day, I'd introduce a scheme that was based on rewarding people for good behaviour. Instead of fining people, I'd provide tax relief to organisations who paid bonuses to their staff who cycled to work. That way, pollution would be reduced and people would get fitter, putting less strain on the NHS and making it cheaper to run,' said Tabitha.

'What they call a win-win situation,' said Eric.

'Exactly that,' said Tabitha.

'It would be difficult to administer,' said Gloria.

'And would there be enough popular support for it, I wonder,' said Andrew.

'I've been given the responsibility for choosing a present for Babaji,' said Geraldine. 'Will you help me?'

'Of course we will,' said Tabitha on behalf of herself and Gloria.

'What are you thinking of getting him?' said Gloria, flapping her big ears.

'A salwar kameez,' said Geraldine.

They went out into the main high street of Mahabalipuram. Andrew came with them to point them in the right direction. The first shop that they came to was like a market stall in that salwar kameezes were hung up outside on coat hangers.

'What about this one?' said Geraldine, pointing to a dark brown salwar kameez. 'We could always have it embroidered with his name in pink.'

'We could,' said Tabitha, a little unenthusiastic about the colour choice, which matched his skin.

Waving her trunk, Gloria hissed at her.

'What about this for Andrew?' She pointed to a bolt of bright yellow raw silk.

'Where is he?' said Tabitha in a whisper.

'It's all right, he's gone back to the hotel,' said Gloria.

'Phew,' said Tabitha. 'But why yellow for him and brown for Babaji?'

Gloria took the bolt of yellow raw silk to the till. Tabitha noticed a black silk salwar kameez embroidered with red drops of blood, like Durga.

'How much?' she asked the shopkeeper.

'Seven hundred rupees,' said the shopkeeper, showing her to a changing room with a green velvet curtain.

Tabitha tried it on. It was a perfect fit. On her way to the till, she noticed two more salwaar kameezes. One was pale grey with dark grey circles and the other was striped in autumnal shades. Perfect for the elephant and the glang, she thought. Tabitha suggested they try them on. They did so and, to her delight, they acquired them too. Tabitha wondered if Andrew would be pleased when he saw his three favourite animals dressed in such fitting salwar kameezes.

Afterwards they got a tuk-tuk back to the hotel. Gloria and Tabitha went for a dip in the sea followed by a walk along the beach where, in a small fishing village, they met a well-spoken Indian called Mathi Vann who asked them to visit his home the following morning. They accepted his kind invitation.

Back at the hotel, Tabitha returned to their room via the hotel shop, where she bought a sequined cushion cover and a moonstone necklace. She took a shower and rang room service for a hairdryer. She dried her fur, put on her new salwar kameez and moonstone necklace, and applied some make-up. Gloria did the same, and they went to the terrace and found themselves a seat. Tracey appeared wearing her lime green sari embroidered with gold, her ruby and diamond pendant and a pair of brown leather sandals that had seen better days. Tabitha nearly got the giggles.

'Would you like a drink, memsahib?' said the waiter.

'Yes please,' Tabitha said, spluttering. 'A mineral water.'

While Gloria and Tracey were in conversation, Tabitha reflected that Eastern women were like pencils. They propelled themselves using the lower part of their bodies, occasionally exposing their ankles and feet. Western women, and bison for that matter, were square by comparison, using their entire anatomies to propel themselves. They looked as if they were about to trip over their saris at any moment.

After they had had their dinner from the buffet, on her way to get dessert, Tabitha passed Andrew and he whispered, 'If you'd like to come to room 25 in the main part of the hotel above the kitchen later this evening, you'd be most welcome.'

Tabitha finished her trifle as quickly as she could. But Andrew started another conversation. Tabitha could hardly believe her ears. Why had he started another conversation when he could have been upstairs with her? Especially yet another conversation with Henry and Geraldine on the subject of why we exist. Could be a very long conversation indeed. Henry said something that implied the inferiority of the female sex. Tabitha put him to rights in no uncertain terms and, eventually, Andrew said his goodnights, giving Geraldine an unnecessarily warm hug in Tabitha's view.

She got into bed and read. Gloria read, then she turned out the light.

'Night night,' said Tabitha.

'Night night,' said Gloria.

Tabitha allowed enough time for all the hotel guests to take to their beds, then she got out of hers. 'I'm just going for a walk,' she whispered.

Gloria, bless her, said nothing.

With her heart pounding in the back of her throat, Tabitha crept round the hotel looking for room 25. Eventually she found a set of stairs leading to some rooms above the kitchen. Outside one of them was a neatly arranged pair of Andrew's Russell & Bromley brown leather sandals. She knocked gently. No answer. She knocked again. This time he came to the door wearing a sarong tied round his waist. His state of half-undress took Tabitha aback. With her hand in his, he led her into the room and they sat on the edge of the bed.

'I'm glad you decided to come,' he said.

Why wouldn't I, she thought.

With his head on the headboard, he reclined. 'Why don't you join me?' He showered her with little kisses all over her face. Then he cuddled her.

'How was it for you?' he asked.

'What?' she said.

'The tour, of course,' he said.

'Oh,' she said. She told him about the difficulties of being a single tigress on tour, accused of causing arguments between the hoolocks, stared at with daggers by Tracey every time Eric talked to her…etcetera.

'Who did you find the most challenging?'

'It's a hard call, but probably Kathleen.'

'Why do you say that?'

'She was always following me, copying me, and I didn't like that.'

Andrew listened to every word Tabitha had to say, then he made love to her. When they'd finished making love, he said, 'There, there,' as if he was trying to comfort her.

'There's no need to comfort me,' she said.

'There, there,' he said.

After a while, she asked, 'How am I going to return to my room and face Gloria?'

'Don't forget, you're a forty something tigress. You can do as you like,' he said.

'I still hate having to be economical with the truth with Gloria – she's my friend.'

'There's no need to feel guilty. If you're quiet as a church mouse, she won't even notice you coming back.'

'I guess so,' she said, unconvinced.

She never did find out whether Gloria was asleep or pretending to be.

CHAPTER 25

For the last time, Tabitha packed her small green bag and put it outside the door. At breakfast she ordered banana fritters. Gloria had a headache and didn't feel able to visit the well-spoken Mathi Vann, so Tabitha went on her own.

She met him at the hotel gate and they walked along the beach in a northerly direction, past fishing boats made from the hollowed-out trunks of coconut palms. With the sand between her toes, jungle to her left, the angled waves of the Bay of Bengal to her right, blue sky overhead and the occasional brown cow passing by, and with love in her heart, she was in heaven. Heading inland, they came to a small temple with three shrines. At the second of the three shrines, dedicated to Hanuman the monkey god, Tabitha heard a human cry. Andrew had spoken of out-of-body experiences and she wondered if it was him trying to communicate with her.

Inside, the temple was full of fishing nets. Tabitha was reminded of a project she had once done to evaluate the use of toilet blocks by local animals who needed somewhere to store their bicycles and used the toilet blocks for this purpose.

She wondered if Andrew knew that one of his beloved temples was being used to store fishing nets, and resolved to ask him.

Mathi Vann took her to a small courtyard surrounded by dilapidated buildings.

'This is where we used to live,' he said. 'It was built by the local government using inappropriate building materials.'

'I'll say.'

They next arrived at a small hut with a thatched roof, and went in. The floor of the one room was made from dried mud and there was a small kitchen area, also made from dried mud. There were no beds, just a couple of sleeping bags and a neatly rolled mat. In the corner of the room, there was a small black and white telly. It was on.

'Manchester United versus Arsenal,' said Mathi Vann.

An elderly woman stirred a pot in the kitchen. 'This is my mother,' said Mathi Vann.

'Delighted to meet you,' said Tabitha.

A beautiful young woman entered the hut.

'And this is my sister,' said Mathi Vann.

His mother made Tabitha a cup of tea and they took their leave to visit a local school, where the excited children asked, 'Have you got any pens?'

Tabitha didn't.

They returned to the beach, and as the sand got hot Mathi Vann offered Tabitha his flip-flops, which she accepted. It was a kind offer. They crossed the scrub at the back of the beach and came to a dell surrounded by Corsican pines.

'The temple of Saluvankuppam,' said Mathi Vann. 'And this is the tiger cave.'

As well as being a tigress, Tabitha was born in the year of the tiger, and she felt enormously at home. She was loath to leave.

They walked back down the beach. Tabitha asked Mathi Vann about the history of a big modern house they were passing.

'It was built for a German woman,' he said. 'If you like, I could build you a house.'

'What would it be like?'

'Like my house,' he said.

Tabitha wondered about the possibility of moving to India as they walked back to the hotel. Mathi Vann gave her his postal address and email.

'Send my regards to your mother and your sister,' she said, promising to write, send biros for the children and, God willing, one day to return.

Andrew and Tabitha saw each other in England three times only. The first time he came to her house wearing a leather jacket, which smelt of Indian spices. They kissed behind the door, in the kitchen and in the bedroom. Afterwards he wanted Marmite on toast.

'There isn't any Marmite, I'm afraid,' said Tabitha.

'Go downstairs and see,' he said. She went downstairs into the kitchen. There, sure enough, was Marmite staring her in the face.

As they left the house together, he said that he felt like a teenager in love. It was early March, there was a cold north wind, but the sun was shining and she was wearing her Mongolian sheepskin jacket.

'Me too,' she said.

The second time, he came to lunch and was decidedly off, especially in the bathroom, where she showed him the strings of shells she had bought in India and which were now hanging from the ceiling to form a 'curtain' at the side of the bath.

The last time, they went to Brighton together. She was working and her meeting finished early. She telephoned Andrew at home to let him know they could hit the road. He was engaged on the phone. She felt annoyed that he hadn't even left the house.

When she got in his car, which also smelt of Indian spices, he kissed her on the cheek. Something was wrong. They didn't talk about it – just proceeded to Brighton, where they met with some of his friends and had lunch in an Indian restaurant. Afterwards they walked down to the beach. With his brown lace-up shoes, he found it hard walking on the pebbles. They sat down. She expected him to put his arm around her, but he didn't.

On the way back to London he asked her about her other travels, and she told him about Antarctica and getting chucked off the boat.

'You should write it all down,' he said.

She didn't tell him about the diary she'd written in India. She did tell John. Remember her friend John? She and John picked up where she and Andrew left off.

'Keep the powder dry,' said John. And so she did, 'til now.